BREAKING
DOWN
VONNEGUT

BREAKING
DOWN
VONNEGUT

JULIA A. WHITEHEAD

JB JOSSEY-BASS™
A Wiley Brand

Jossey-Bass
A Wiley Imprint
111 River St, Hoboken, NJ 07030
www.josseybass.com

Jossey-Bass books and products are available through most bookstores. To contact Jossey-Bass directly, call our Customer Care Department within the U.S. at 800–956–7739, outside the U.S. at +1 317 572 3986, or fax +1 317 572 4002.

Wiley also publishes its books in a variety of electronic formats and by print-on-demand. Some material included with standard print versions of this book may not be included in e-books or in print-on-demand. If this book refers to media such as a CD or DVD that is not included in the version you purchased, you may download this material at http://booksupport.wiley.com. For more information about Wiley products, visit www.wiley.com.

Library of Congress Cataloging-in-Publication Data

Names: Whitehead, Julia A., author.
Title: Breaking down Vonnegut / Julia A. Whitehead.
Description: Hoboken, NJ : Jossey-Bass, 2022. | Includes bibliographical references and index.
Identifiers: LCCN 2021055854 (print) | LCCN 2021055855 (ebook) | ISBN 9781119746096 (paperback) | ISBN 9781119746195 (adobe pdf) | ISBN 9781119746157 (epub)
Subjects: LCGFT: Literary criticism.
Classification: LCC PS3572.O5 Z95 2022 (print) | LCC PS3572.O5 (ebook) | DDC 813/.54 [B]—dc23/eng/20211221
LC record available at https://lccn.loc.gov/2021055854
LC ebook record available at https://lccn.loc.gov/2021055855

Cover Art & Design: Paul McCarthy

SKY10032255_123021

To my children, Daniel and Joseph

Contents

About the Author

Julia A. Whitehead, an award-winning entrepreneur, is the founder and CEO of the Kurt Vonnegut Museum and Library in Indianapolis, celebrating its tenth anniversary. Whitehead is a recognized expert and lecturer on the life and works of Kurt Vonnegut. Her writing has appeared in the *Chicago Tribune*, Biography.com, *So It Goes*, and *Finding the Words: Stories and Poems by Women Veterans*. She has held writing and editing positions with Random House, Inc., Military Officers Association of America, and the state legislatures of South Carolina and Indiana. Whitehead taught English in Thailand in 2000 and worked as a medical writer for Eli Lilly and Co. In this capacity, Whitehead also represented Lilly as an adjunct professor of Medical Writing and Editing at Florida A&M University. Whitehead holds a bachelor's degree in English from the University of South Carolina and a master's degree in International Relations from University of Indianapolis. She is a member of the Indianapolis Consortium of Arts Administrators and the Affiliate Steering Committee for Chicago's American Writers Museum. Whitehead led the creation of the *So It Goes* literary journal, the inclusion of the Vonnegut Library as an official national location of Literary Landmarks of the American Library Association, and the development of the Vonnegut Youth Writing Program serving Indianapolis youth in partnership with the International Alliance of Youth Writing Centers. She served as an officer in the US Marine Corps. A documentary film she wrote, produced, and directed titled *My Friend Mickey* was featured in the 2018 Heartland Film Festival and was a finalist for best documentary in the Los Angeles Love International Film Festival. She is the proud mother of sons Daniel and Joseph.

About the Kurt Vonnegut Museum and Library

The Kurt Vonnegut Museum and Library (KVML) is a public-benefit, nonprofit organization located at 543 Indiana Ave., in Indianapolis. Its mission is to champion the legacy of Kurt Vonnegut and the principles of free expression and common decency. The flat-iron style building (so-called because of its triangular shape) was placed on the National Register of Historic Places in 1987. Built on land once belonging to Native Americans, the structure was erected in 1882 in a neighborhood occupied at that time mostly by German Americans, Irish Americans, Eastern Europeans, and African Americans. During the first half of the twentieth century, it achieved historic significance as part of African American culture in the Historic Indiana Avenue Cultural District. In 2022, a year celebrating Vonnegut's 100th birthday, this building was selected to receive the first designation for a Literary Landmark in the State of Indiana on the National Register administered by the American Library Association.

The 10,400-square-foot building serves as a community arts center featuring a Youth Writing Program for local high school students, artist and author events, freedom of expression events, musical and comedy performances, virtual programming for a global audience, and a gift shop that can be found online at vonnegutlibrary.org. The building houses a library and museum filled with artifacts, books, and artwork that the late Kurt Vonnegut acquired or created throughout his life. For more information or to support the organization with a donation, visit www.vonnegutlibrary.org or write to Julia.whitehead@vonnegut-library.org.

Acknowledgments

I would like to thank my publisher, Jossey-Bass, a division of Wiley, and especially Riley Harding and Christine O'Connor, for choosing me for this project. I have always wanted to write this book. Thanks to Cheryl Ferguson, Mary Beth Rosswurm, and Ashante Thomas for your careful and thoughtful work.

Mark Vonnegut took a call from me more than ten years ago. I rambled on about how I had an idea for a museum and library. Mark gave me a chance. He introduced me to Don and Annie Farber. Don was Vonnegut's long-time attorney and remained in that capacity after Vonnegut's death. Had Mark and Don not believed in our mission and our intentions, there would be no Vonnegut Library. I've had the privilege of reading Mark's books and serving on panel discussions with Mark. His support for our work is greatly appreciated.

A hearty thanks to Vonnegut's daughters Lily, Edith (Edie), and Nanette (Nanny, or as Vonnegut wrote in a letter, "Dearest of all possible Nans"). The memories and thoughts that you share enrich the study of Vonnegut. I appreciate your details that show Vonnegut as a real person – imperfect and wonderful. I treasure you.

My colleague Tom Roston, a journalist and author of the book *The Writer's Crusade: Kurt Vonnegut and the Many Lives of Slaughterhouse-Five*, wrote to me after reviewing some of my chapters: "Welcome to the club." I assume he was referring to those who are fascinated with Vonnegut, obsessed with research about him, write about him, and share their writing with the world. I am grateful to Tom and also to Rodney Allen, James Alexander Thom, and Brian Welke for carefully reviewing chapters of my book. I am also thankful for members of "the club" with whom I have befriended, commiserated, quoted, sought advice, and celebrated, including Marc Leeds, A'Lelia Bundles, Drew DeSimone, Lewis Black, Robert Basler, Christina Jarvis, Ginger Strand, David Brancaccio, John Green, David Hoppe, Dave Eggers, Steve Groner Ellerhoff, Dan Wakefield, Dan Simon, Scott Vonnegut, Suzanne McConnell, Tom Marvin, Terrian Barnes, Kevin Finch, Sophie Maurer, Susan Farrell, Joe Petro, Greg Sumner, John Krull, and Hugh Vandivier.

I owe a debt of gratitude to the staff of the Kurt Vonnegut Museum and Library, and especially Chris Lafave. The board of directors also deserve acknowledgment – not only for what they do to carry on Vonnegut's legacy but also for recognizing that I have creative energy to complete projects outside of my workday.

Thanks to Kurt Vonnegut, whom I never met, for being an inspiration, a survivor, a messenger – and a funny one at that.

Those whose lives were impacted while I've been distracted with writing include my mom and my children, Joseph and Daniel White-head. I'm grateful for your encouragement and for giving me the time to write. Thanks for being extraordinary souls who believe we can do anything we set our minds to create.

This book could not have been created without the support of Janie and Mickey Maurer. Janie was there when it counted the most, and Mickey, a most careful editor, made this book readable from one draft to another. He listened to my squeaking about this concern or that. Sometimes I think he unwittingly willed it into existence, because two days after he asked if I had ever thought of writing a book about Vonnegut, I received a call from my publisher describing the project. That's deep magic.

Introduction

Kurt Vonnegut fanatics from around the world cut the ribbon on donated storefront space to dedicate the Kurt Vonnegut Museum and Library (KVML) in Indianapolis in 2011. I am the founder of this organization. As this book goes to print, we are celebrating 10 years at KVML. I was a medical writer for the pharmaceutical giant Eli Lilly and Co., an officer in the United States Marine Corps, an editor for Random House Publishing, and a teacher of English to 100 second graders in Bangkok, Thailand. My interest in biography was sparked in childhood after reading about Eleanor Roosevelt. In the Marine Corps, I was assigned to the Marine Corps Research Center and worked with the biographies and archival collections of Marines. When I worked at Eli Lilly, I volunteered as a "corporate ambassador" conducting guests tours of the replica of Col. Eli Lilly's original post–Civil War building and teaching visitors about the drug-making process and materials used at the time. I became an expert on Col. Eli Lilly, and as a former Marine I became fascinated with stories of his military experience, including his time as a prisoner of war held by the Confederate army.

Col. Lilly held my interest, but the death of another prisoner of war captured my thoughts in 2007. That was the World War II veteran, writer, artist, humorist, car salesman, journalist, corporate public relations writer, and dilettante gambler at the horse track – Kurt Vonnegut. I never met Vonnegut. He was supposed to visit Indianapolis in 2007 during the city's Year of Vonnegut, but he passed away on April 11 after getting tangled up in his dog's leash and falling from the steps of his New York City brownstone.

When I established KVML as a grassroots "club" in 2008 and then a full-blown nonprofit in 2011, I imagined that I would spend days poring over documents, presenting to schools and libraries, and facilitating book clubs' discussions. While I occasionally do that, it became clear within the first month on the job that these tasks that I considered to be most rewarding were not how I would spend most of my time. I had to lead the organization, manage the staff and work with the board, build a strong foundation, mount programs and exhibitions that visitors would enjoy, and figure out how to raise the money to keep all of this going, while also raising funds to someday buy a building, a home – "Kurt's Forever Home." We had big dreams and minimal cash.

Each time I encountered new information on Vonnegut, a new book, article, or donated artifacts or materials, I filed it away for the day when I could devote time to write a book about all I learned. I never got less busy, but finally I decided that during this tenth anniversary year for the KVML leading into the anniversary of Vonnegut's 100th birthday, it is time to share what I've learned. The public's hunger for Vonnegut has never abated.

During the first few years of the KVML, I assumed that at some point I would uncover unflattering information about Vonnegut. While I did encounter one source that was proven to be factually incorrect and salacious, to my surprise, the information shared with me by friends, family, colleagues, and others only endeared me to Vonnegut – not because he was perfect but because he was lovable.

This book is divided into four parts: Part One is 1922–1944, Vonnegut's formative years; Part Two focuses on 1944–1945, the turning-point year of his life; Part Three features his years with his first wife, Jane, and includes three of his early works (*Player Piano*, "Harrison Bergeron," and *Slaughterhouse-Five*); and Part Four highlights the last 35 years of his life with his second wife, Jill. The book relates the Vonnegut story in large part using Vonnegut's own words. The collection of Kurt's letters, edited by Dan Wakefield, and Vonnegut's love letters to his girlfriend and wife-to-be Jane Cox collected by his daughter Edith Vonnegut and other source materials were liberally used and quoted. Source materials by my fellow Vonnegut scholars are cited and appreciated.

There are no villains in this book because, as Kurt wrote in *Slaughterhouse-Five,* "Another thing they [professors at the University of Chicago] taught was that no one was ridiculous or bad or disgusting. Shortly before my father died, he said to me, 'You know – you never wrote a story with a villain in it.' I told him that was one of the things I learned in college after the war."

Some books on the market about Vonnegut are heavily focused on his writing career or story analysis. While I relied on several of these books and his own stories for information and analysis, on those occasions when I interact with the public in discussion about his work, I often recall the stories I've been told over these years in my direct conversations with his friends, children, cousins, nephews, and grand-children. I have shared Vonnegut as a student, father, Army buddy, husband, and friend.

Often, the women in the lives of famous men – or any men – are portrayed as "crazy," jealous, materialistic, or feuding rather than full and complete human beings with intelligence, emotional maturity, and kindness. In my book, the women in Vonnegut's life receive the weight they deserve.

I have devoted the past ten years of my professional life to the study of Vonnegut and the promotion of his work and ideas. If this book portrays Vonnegut in a light that is more positive than you would like, perhaps you can forgive me for that. From the grave, he charmed me.

BREAKING
DOWN
VONNEGUT

PART I

Young Kurt Vonnegut was somewhat of a heartthrob. Shortridge High School's "Uglyman" contest ironically highlighted the best-looking and most popular. These artifacts are on display at the Kurt Vonnegut Museum and Library in Indianapolis. Photo courtesy of KVML Curator Chris Lafave.

Chapter One

There Was Always Someone to Talk with, to Play with, to Learn From

Literary luminaries including Emily Dickinson, Herman Melville, Edgar Allan Poe, and Zora Neal Hurston became famous in the world of arts and letters only after they died. Kurt Vonnegut achieved fame during his lifetime, and his literary legacy catapulted him into the ranks of those in world literature who had at least one book that will leave its mark on the world for generations of readers. Sun Tzu, Charles Dickens, Leo Tolstoy, James Joyce, Anne Frank, Mary Shelley, Maya Angelou, and many others deemed the most famous authors in history captured the human condition – each in his or her own way. *Slaughterhouse-Five* is that one book for Vonnegut. Unlike Sun Tzu's *Art of War*, *Slaughterhouse-Five* is a lesson in why there should be an Art of Peace. And why not Vonnegut, a soldier who learned first-hand about war's devastation.

Speaking to his readers as a fellow reader, the common man, Vonnegut was utterly uncommon. He was a soldier, journalist, artist, scholar, author, teacher, humorist, car salesman, public relations lackey, and a voice of multiple generations. His books have sold millions of copies. Vonnegut was recognized with countless awards during his lifetime. His list of accolades is long and impressive. He served in prestigious professorships at Harvard, Smith College, and the Iowa Writers Workshop, among others, yet, despite several attempts, he never received a college degree until honorary degrees were bestowed on him following his writing success. During his first attempt at a college degree, he left school to serve his country during World War II. On his second attempt, he dropped out to get a job to support his new family. For a young man who was raised to believe education was everything, these educational sacrifices did not go unnoticed. Vonnegut's decision to serve in the military and to marry Jane Cox and raise a family gave him the life experiences and support network needed to unleash his brilliant and creative mind on the world. He would later receive multiple honorary degrees from various universities, including Hobart and Smith College, City University of New York, and the University of Chicago.

Vonnegut hailed from German *freethinkers*. His great grandfather, Clemens Vonnegut, born Catholic in 1824, was a "rabble-rouser," who fled religious persecution following his participation in demonstrations for religious freedom in Germany. He married Katarina Blank and enjoyed a successful business life, acquiring sole ownership of a jointly owned hardware enterprise and renaming it Vonnegut Hardware Company, a local favorite until 1965, when the company was sold, with the new owners keeping the name. Clemens became a leader on the Board of School Commissioners in Indianapolis, and, with his family, engaged in creating a German freethinkers community in Indianapolis.

The concept of "freethinkers" today is closely related to humanism. In his book *Timequake*, Vonnegut wrote, "Humanists try to behave decently and honorably without any expectation of rewards or punishments in an afterlife. The creator of the Universe [sic] has been to us unknowable so far. We serve as well as we can the highest abstraction of which we have some understanding, which is our community."[1]

Vonnegut's paternal grandparents, Bernard Vonnegut and Nanette Schnull Vonnegut, perpetuated the family's tradition of freethinking. Bernard established an architecture firm, Vonnegut and Bohn. Their interest in the arts, enhanced by Nanette's education in music and literature, was imparted on son Kurt Vonnegut Sr., who carried on the family tradition of community engagement and enjoyment of the arts. He also led the family architecture business. His son, Kurt Jr., appreciated his family's contributions to the Indianapolis architectural landscape. His fondest childhood memories related to the home his father designed for his family, which included Kurt Jr.'s two older siblings, Bernard and Alice. Vonnegut's mother, Edith, was the cultured daughter of a beer-brewing family. After her death in 1944 from an overdose of prescription medication, Vonnegut wrote: "It is rather for us, the living, to be here dedicated – and dedicated we are, Bernard, Alice and Kay, to those elements of our mother which were her birthright: complete and unself devotion to her family morality; inflexible sense of fair play; childlike love for all things alive."[2]

Vonnegut was born on November 11, 1922, celebrated then as Armistice Day, a day of peace. On the surface, Vonnegut's childhood in Indianapolis was idyllic and did not prepare him for the challenges he faced in his early twenties. While it is clear from letters written during his early life that he enjoyed nearly everything a child needs to be physically and emotionally healthy, he did not escape the childhood fears and worries about home or school. A closer look reveals a boy who was bullied by classmates yet seen by others as funny, smart, handsome, and the life-of-the-party. His childhood – enriched but also requiring hard work and accountability – allowed him to survive later tragedies and maintain his spirit and faith in humanity. Vonnegut possessed a curiosity about a higher power, at times denying and at times embracing its existence, a contradiction that many humans experience.

His formative years were spent with friends and a large extended family, visits to nature, and a commendable public-school education at Shortridge High School in Indianapolis, which published the only daily high school newspaper in America at the time. Vonnegut served as one of its editors. As an adult, he became a journalist, capitalizing on the same skills present in Vonnegut even as a child: his ability to observe and eloquently and accurately assess people and situations – the human condition.

While his parents loved one another, they were not a happy couple. External circumstances related to the Great Depression and the loss of much of their wealth; the mistreatment of German Americans, which began during World War I; and the fears and challenges brought on by World War II exacerbated the internal demands that they – like all parents – faced when trying to raise a family. Unlike most families, Vonnegut's family could afford to provide jobs for household servants. Ida Young, a grandchild of slaves, became the family's cook and inspired ideas and characters in some of the books that made Vonnegut famous. She was the person he came home to after school each day to talk about his day. From the Bible stories she told and the stories of historical struggles of the African American community, he learned about ancient and more recent slavery and racial segregation. He memorized a passage from The Lord's Prayer that he often quoted when giving graduation speeches years after achieving success: "Forgive us our trespasses as we forgive those who trespass against us." This quotation both served him and helped him understand the loving kindness expressed by Mrs. Young. His concern for the human condition stemmed, in part, from knowing and loving her. Vonnegut wrote of her in the Preface of his book *Wampeters, Fomas, and Grandfalloons*: "At least I am aware of my origins – in a big, brick dreamhouse designed by my architect father, where nobody was home for long periods of time, except for me and Ida Young." Vonnegut said, "Ida Young, in combination with my Uncle Alex, had as much to do with my upbringing as my parents did."[3]

Vonnegut's Uncle Alex was a kind-hearted individual with whom Vonnegut spent many hours learning about the world and observing the unconditional love his uncle shared in his marriage. Uncle Alex and his wife Raye – their strong bond and kind, affectionate behavior – was a welcome contrast to the difficult yet committed relationship Vonnegut observed with his parents. Vonnegut was curious about human relationships and especially after he began dating as a teenager. The strength he developed during this time and his belief in the innate goodness of humans gave him the fortitude he needed to survive the worst human treatment he faced as a young adult during World War II.

Throughout Vonnegut's adult life – in his speeches and interviews and in his books – the theme of Eden is ever present. Aspects of Vonnegut's childhood created a memorable Eden. These include an extended family, a sense of religious freedom and meaningful discussions with adults about topics of God and humanism, common decency that is often reflected in the term *Midwest values,* the importance of meaningful work, and a solid education including both school and community assets such as a strong public library system and a sense of sticking together through difficult times. In one interview, Vonnegut said: "We all should have extended families. We need them, just like we need vitamins and minerals. And most of us don't have those extended families anymore. I had one in Indianapolis, when I was born, which was in 1922. I had uncles and aunts all over the place, and cousins, family businesses that I could go into, whole rows of cottages that were full of my relatives. There was always someone to talk with, to play with, to learn from."[4]

Vonnegut's older brother, Bernard, remained a friend throughout his life but Vonnegut was especially close to Alice. She was the middle child and was his playmate. Vonnegut's books *Timequake* and *Slapstick* include examples of their strong friendship.

The Vonnegut clan owned as many as twelve homes on a lake north of Indianapolis, Lake Maxincuckee. The original home was built by Vonnegut's great-grandfather Clemens in 1889 as a family retreat. "We went out in an old, leaky rowboat, which all my life I had called *The Beralikur*, a mixture of my first name with those of my siblings Bernard and Alice. But that name was not painted on the boat, which would have been redundant. Everybody who was anybody at Maxincuckee already knew that the name of that leaky boat was *the Beralikur*."[5]

Vonnegut's childhood included countless social events with family and conversations about religion, the arts, politics, and education with creative minds of the time from progressive leaders including two socialism advocates who were political powerhouses and union organizers, Powers Hapgood and Eugene V. Debs (whom Vonnegut wrote about in his book *Jailbird*) and the popular novelist Booth Tarkington. Young Vonnegut's life was filled with festive times at the Athenaeum (a large building designed by his grandfather to house a German-American cultural/social community center), and outdoor activities from Lake Maxincuckee to his teenage "prairie trek" to western states with a group of boys and a guide with experience as a Scout leader who taught them how to live off the land.

Within homes and in public venues, dancing was a popular social activity among the Vonnegut family. Vonnegut was born the same year as the popular dance, the Charleston, hit the scene. During the Roaring

Twenties and most of Vonnegut's twentieth-century life, people danced. In his book *A Man Without a Country*, Vonnegut wrote: "We are dancing animals."[6] His family and his relatives and friends had dance floors in their homes. Some rolled back the carpet; others had a dedicated ballroom. Imagine an entire room of a family home dedicated to a wide-open space where scads of people would gather and dance with anybody and everybody. In public places, there were *dance cards* that included the names of the individuals with whom a woman would dance on a particular night. It was considered impolite to turn down an invitation to dance and was done only in the event that another invitation had been received first. ("I'll pencil you in" was a happy response to an invitation; "Sorry, my dance card is full" could result in great disappointment.) While it is unfortunate that American society largely abandoned an emphasis on public and private-event dancing, the expectation that women dance with just anybody who asks was a tradition that thankfully went by the wayside.

Amidst the fun, there was pain. The bullying that Vonnegut experienced culminated with him being jammed into a trash can by high school athletes, and his home life was upsetting as the family began to experience the misfortune most Americans suffered during the Great Depression and additional financial problems unique to their situation. Scholar Suzanne McConnell wrote, "When his parents lost their fortune through investing in a Ponzi scheme during the Great Depression, she [Vonnegut's mother] tried earning money by writing for magazines."[7] Despite her ability, Edith Vonnegut was unsuccessful in her writing career.

While Vonnegut began his elementary education at the prestigious private institution, Orchard School (where he met Jane Cox, who became his first wife), the loss of his family's wealth during the Great Depression caused him to be transferred to a public elementary school. Vonnegut's stellar experience in the Indianapolis Public School system led Vonnegut to advocate for funding and other support for public schools. "I thought we should be the envy of the world with our public schools. And I went to such a public school. So I knew that such a school was possible. . . . And, my God, we had a daily paper, we had a debating team, had a fencing team. We had a chorus, a jazz band, a serious orchestra. And all this with a Great Depression going on. And I wanted everybody to have such a school."[8]

The education system in a community is just one aspect of development that contributes to a sense of place. A sense of place – home – mattered to Vonnegut and served as a theme in his writing and speeches. The values he learned in Indianapolis and his appreciation of his formative years led him to write about the city often – sometimes critically, sometimes lovingly – but always as a point of discussion. Later in life, he said, "All of my jokes are Indianapolis. My attitudes are Indianapolis. My adenoids are Indianapolis. What people like about me is Indianapolis. If I ever severed myself from Indianapolis, I would be out of business."[9]

Vonnegut wanted Indiana – and Indianapolis specifically – to be more progressive. He found its racial segregation unacceptable. He mocked its often-conservative approach to social issues and made teasing comments about those citizens whom he thought had backward ideas, but he believed in "Hoosier Hospitality," a warm-hearted way of treating strangers. He wrote in a 1987 letter: "I would welcome the opportunity to kill the canard that I scorn my hometown, which gave so much to me. Although I live in the east, I remain an aggressively and sometimes abrasively Indianapolis person and will remain such until I die."[10]

Being a "Middle Westerner" was a point of pride to him. "Thus, do I and millions like me tell strangers that we are Middle Westerners, as though we deserved some kind of a medal for being that."[11]

The summer after his senior year of high school, Vonnegut vacationed in the White Mountains of New Hampshire with his brother, but his carefree, childhood days would soon take a serious turn.

PART II

Kurt Vonnegut's official military photo was taken following his enlistment in the U.S. Army in 1943. Copyright © 2020 by Kurt Vonnegut LLC, used by permission of The Wylie Agency LLC.

Chapter Two

I Look Sort of Starved

Vonnegut graduated from Shortridge High School in 1940. He entered Cornell University that fall with doubts about his choice for a university (he had options) and a major, but the Delta Upsilon fraternity made his transition easier. Grades were relegated to second or third priority behind his fraternity and the pursuit of his passion, journalism, serving on the staff of the *Cornell Daily Sun* while continuing to study science. When the Japanese bombed Pearl Harbor in 1941, Vonnegut, who previously held his family's isolationist views regarding American involvement in the war, felt a sense of patriotic responsibility.

Within the next year and following a bout of pneumonia, Vonnegut left Cornell to enlist in the Army. His parents were not pleased. Enlisted men with no college degree would have fewer options with regard to assignments by military leadership and fewer opportunities for professional growth and development. Also, in the event of capture, enlisted servicemembers experienced harsher treatment at the hands of the enemy. The choice to enlist as a "regular" soldier was another defining moment of Vonnegut's life, a choice that caused greater suffering but, he later said, greater pride because it gave him the experience of connecting with those who were, because of class discrimination, expected to withstand more pain. Throughout his life, Vonnegut went back and forth between wanting to be among the elite and wanting to be, as he once wrote in a private correspondence, "just plain folks." Raised in a family where being "average" was not particularly acceptable, Vonnegut wrestled with this throughout his life, the urge to fit in among the elite and the urge to fit in among "just plain folks" – sometimes fearing that he might be "just plain folks."[1]

While many enlisted soldiers have no education beyond high school, the fact that Vonnegut was studying science at Cornell, his military aptitude test scores, and his advanced communication skills initially led him away from the military specialty assignment most soldiers expected to receive: infantry. Vonnegut was sent to Carnegie Institute of Technology to study mechanical engineering. He then was transferred to the University of Tennessee to finish his coursework, but by the spring of 1944, this special training program was canceled.[2]

Vonnegut had a girl "back home." He was madly in love with his childhood sweetheart, Jane Cox. Jane's father, Thomas Harvey Cox, was a lawyer and her mother, Riah Fagan Leonard, was an authority in classical literature. She co-authored a book on grammar for teachers called *General Language* that was read in Europe as well as America. Jane was well read with excellent skills in writing and editing. While Vonnegut was at Cornell, Jane attended Swarthmore College, but the distance between them didn't keep the two apart. Their relationship was passionate. Vonnegut wrote to Jane of her beauty but also raved about her creativity and intelligence.

During this period, they did not demand fidelity, but Vonnegut regularly wrote that he intended to marry Jane. He predicted they would have seven children. The chemistry between the two was just the fire that Vonnegut wanted and needed to carry him through a time when American life was fraught with fear of additional enemy attacks at home and abroad and the constant scarcity of various products and foods because of the war effort. Vonnegut's weekends with Jane and their steamy correspondence satisfied many of his physical and emotional needs: "The young and warmly loving two of us in bed are closer to God than the topmost spires of the greatest and most blessed cathedral in creation."[3]

One letter written while Vonnegut was still at Cornell foretold Vonnegut's future profession but also revealed a unique characteristic that led him to capture readers' imagination. "I'm glad I dabbled in the sciences, for I can understand and interpret a great and interesting number of things which would otherwise be forever mysterious. Such a scientific sympathy is, I think, certainly in keeping with the times. Through it my chances as a journalist are enhanced."[4]

Vonnegut's interest in writing as a profession was evident, but his letters also show that both he and Jane saw a future together that would include a great deal of discussions and experiences of theater, literature, music, art, and philosophy. Their daughter Nanette said in an interview: "These were incredibly romantic people who believed in the arts. What my mother and father stressed was that the arts were not an extra-curricular activity; it was fundamental to them. It was how you become more human."[5]

Vonnegut's thoughts about the human condition and the role of community continued and later appeared in his fiction, essays, and speeches: "Through the history of mankind, this question has been asked – Why are we here, and what makes us act as we do? Religion after religion has formed in a fruitless attempt to find some answer."[6]

Meaning-of-life questions became more pronounced for Vonnegut during the most tumultuous year of his life, spring 1944–spring 1945. On Mother's Day weekend at age 21, when Vonnegut came home while on military leave, he and his sister found their mother dead from an overdose of barbiturates, prescribed by her doctor for anxiety and sleeplessness. Although there is no conclusive evidence to prove it was more than an accidental overdose, Vonnegut often said in interviews that she died from suicide. Vonnegut was devastated. He clung to Jane even more.

"I need someone to tell me big wonderful lies about myself – someone to be deeply concerned about me – I want to feel that someone is watching my every move and giving very much of a damn – I want a deep and boundless love that I can brashly abuse and be forgiven for it. These playthings were mine until two weeks ago. I cried for a very long time."[7]

Vonnegut's plea for Jane to be his parental figure and at the same time his lover and friend is something many psychologists and social scientists say all people want all the time throughout life. For the rest of Vonnegut's war, he called on Jane for this unconditional love. Vonnegut wrote about this kind of love in various novels including the World War II story, *Mother Night*.

> No matter what I really was, no matter what I really meant, uncritical love was what I needed – and my Helga was the angel who gave it to me. Copiously.

> No young person on earth is so excellent in all respects as to need no uncritical love. Good Lord – as youngsters play their parts in political tragedies with casts of billions, uncritical love is the only real treasure they can look for.[8]

Vonnegut knew what he wanted from a relationship and wasn't ashamed to ask for it. After graduating from college, Jane was busy with her own professional life, working in Washington, D.C., for the Office of Strategic Services (what later became the CIA) during the war, but she was not about to abandon this lifelong friend-turned-lover during his difficult period.

Having been trained by the military in mechanical engineering, Vonnegut normally would have expected to follow that military career path, but his country was at war. He was reassigned to the 106th Infantry Division, which trained at Camp Atterbury, Indiana. He was being trained as an intelligence scout.

The American war effort needed infantrymen in its last-ditch land effort. He was sent to La Havre, France, and from there his unit transferred to the front lines in Belgium during the Battle of the Bulge. Vonnegut's unit was quickly surrounded by Nazis, who force-marched their captives 60 miles in the snow to board cattle cars to Dresden, Germany. Vonnegut suffered frostbite for which he later received a Purple Heart. Months later, Vonnegut wrote a letter to his family describing the experience:

On Christmas Eve the Royal Air Forced bombed and strafed our unmarked train. They killed about one-hundred-and-fifty of us. We got a little water on Christmas Day and moved slowly across Germany to a large P.O.W. Camp in Muhlburg, south of Berlin. We were released from the box cars on New Year's Day. The Germans herded us through scalding delousing showers. Many men died from the shock of the showers after ten days of starvation, thirst, and exposure. But I didn't.[9]

Vonnegut noted in the letter that officers, per the Geneva Conventions, were not taken as working prisoners. "I am, as you know, a private." This experience of being among the less privileged endeared Vonnegut to "the troops" and them to him. This ability to accurately and poignantly describe the human experience drew his work to the public eye for the next few generations.

When his train, minus the officers who were placed in more comfortable surroundings, finally reached Dresden, Vonnegut and his fellow POWs were housed in building #5, Slaughterhouse-Five, which became the title of his internationally acclaimed war novel (see Chapter Five). While Vonnegut was held by the Nazis, often beaten and malnourished, the Allies, American and British bombers, firebombed Dresden in an effort to finally stop Hitler but also as vengeance for the terror bombings of London. The firebombing lasted for three days and left the flaming city in rubble. Vonnegut and others had been taken underground. He said it sounded like giants were walking above. When he came to the surface at the end of the bombing, he witnessed a horrific scene. Vonnegut's task at this time as a prisoner of war, to burn the victims, which included women, children, pets, the aged, and others, in large funeral pyres, left him convinced war was barbaric and absurd and set the stage for his lifelong plea for common decency and peaceful coexistence. Vonnegut's postwar research led him to believe that 135,000 civilians were killed during the firebombing of Dresden, a number that experts, including author Sinclair McKay as recently as 2020, said was overestimated by possibly 100,000 or more.

When Vonnegut returned from the war, he learned that the American public was never made aware of the firebombing of Dresden. The lack of information would cause him to wonder and search for a proper accounting. According to journalist and author Thomas Roston, Vonnegut was also unaware that factories in Dresden had been retrofitted for the war effort and the city was a hub for transporting German troops, another factor contributing to the decision to target this seemingly peaceful city. In his book, *The Writer's Crusade: Kurt Vonnegut and the Many Lives of Slaughterhouse-Five*, Roston shared the statistics that Vonnegut would not have known at the time:

> On February 13, 1945, eight hundred bombers of the British Royal Air Force rained 1,400 tons of high-explosive bombs over the city, along with more than 1,100 tons of incendiary bombs, which were designed to start fires that ripped through Dresden. Over the next two days, five hundred US planes dropped another thousand tons of explosives on city infrastructure, such as railways and bridges.[10]

The letters Vonnegut wrote while a prisoner likely were not received by their intended recipients, but the letters Vonnegut wrote to Jane during his war years that were collected and saved are a glimpse into the private romantic life of young lovers. They represent the difference between a carefree young man prior to the most difficult year of his life – spring 1944 to spring 1945 – and the young man who suffered from what Vonnegut's son, Dr. Mark Vonnegut, said was likely undiagnosed post-traumatic stress disorder (PTSD).

Matured and hardened, Vonnegut attempted to prevent a lasting desensitization following his experience of tragedy and torture, including physical pain and deprivation. His physical and mental fortitude, bolstered by his foundation in the arts and humanities, allowed him to psychologically survive his war experience. In her book *Kurt Vonnegut: Drawings*, Vonnegut's daughter Nanette wrote that by 1930, Vonnegut had "downloaded everything he needed: Doc [Kurt Sr.'s] and Alice's visual whimsy, Bernard's mad-scientist view from the clouds, his mother's wild idea that writing might be a means to make money, and the secret joy of doodling in a dreadfully serious world."[11]

Vonnegut sometimes laughed or joked when describing this unthinkable cruelty in his interviews and writing, but readers should never mistake his humor for callousness. As Vonnegut said, "Laughs are exactly as honorable as tears. Laughter and tears are both responses to frustration and exhaustion, to the futility of thinking and striving anymore. I myself prefer to laugh, since there is less cleaning up to do afterward."[12]

Within two months of the Dresden firebombing and Hitler's realization that he could no longer win the war, Vonnegut and his fellow prisoners were released. He made his way back to La Havre, France, and eventually home, but he would be unable to leave the war behind. Though he occasionally said otherwise, it was with him for the rest of his life.

(Letter to Jane – May 25, 1945)

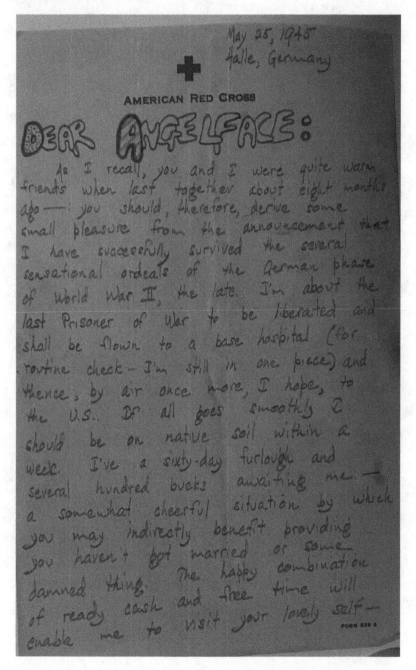

May 25, 1945
Halle, Germany

AMERICAN RED CROSS

DEAR ANGELFACE:

As I recall, you and I were quite warm friends when last together about eight months ago — you should, therefore, derive some small pleasure from the announcement that I have successfully survived the several sensational ordeals of the German phase of World War II, the late. I'm about the last Prisoner of War to be liberated and shall be flown to a base hospital (for routine check — I'm still in one piece) and thence, by air once more, I hope, to the U.S.. If all goes smoothly I should be on native soil within a week. I've a sixty-day furlough and several hundred bucks awaiting me. — a somewhat cheerful situation by which you may indirectly benefit providing you haven't got married or some damned thing. The happy combination of ready cash and free time will enable me to visit your lovely self—

FORM 528 A

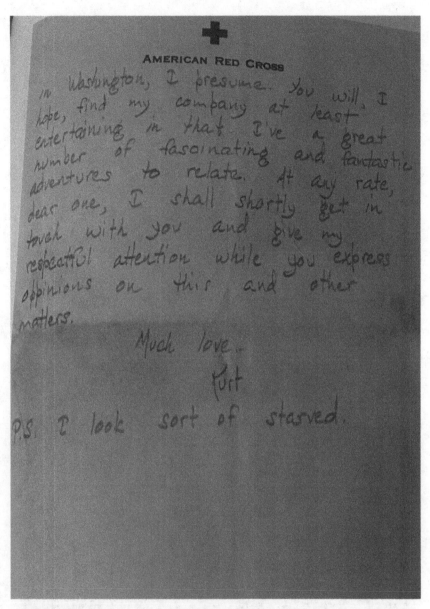

AMERICAN RED CROSS

in Washington, I presume. You will, I hope, find my company at least entertaining in that I've a great number of fascinating and fantastic adventures to relate. At any rate, dear one, I shall shortly get in touch with you and give my respectful attention while you express oppinions on this and other matters.

Much love.

Kurt

P.S. I look sort of starved.

Vonnegut had not completed his required military service, but he was granted military leave and special pay. Before his discharge, following years of courting, he married Jane in September 1945. Jane encouraged him to write during those remainder months in the service. He had shared some of his writing with her over the years, and she recognized his talent, but it was more than that. She was giddy over his writing. She knew his brilliance would be revealed to publishers and editors with a little help. She longed to be his muse, editor, and unofficial agent.

After he finished his stint in the Army, they enrolled at the University of Chicago. Jane studied Russian literature. Kurt studied Anthropology.

"And when I went to the University of Chicago, and I heard the head of the Department of Anthropology, Robert Refield, lecture on the folk society, which was essentially a stable, isolated extended family, he did not have to tell me how nice that could be."[13]

Vonnegut's study of Anthropology was useful for his personal interest and in his writing career. What he learned as a student sparked his imagination, which he revealed in his short stories and novels. He enjoyed his educational experience but felt that he wasn't appreciated:

> I thought a hell of a lot of the University of Chicago, and Chicago didn't think a damn thing about me. I was a very fringe character in the anthropology department. Before Chicago, I had never been a liberal arts or social science major; I'd had chemistry at Cornell. And after Cornell, I was three years in the goddamned infantry in World War II. That tore a big chunk out of my life. The University of Chicago gave returning veterans a test on what they knew generally. They took my credits, which were in physics, chemistry, and math, and admitted me as a graduate student in anthropology. After going through the war and all, I thought man was the thing to study. I really think it ought to be done in second grade, but better in graduate school than nowhere else. And it was interesting.[14]

When Jane became pregnant and dropped out of school, Vonnegut also dropped out of school and began working as a reporter for the Chicago News Bureau, covering the crime beat. City crimes were upsetting but were not the large-scale bombing and other crimes against humanity Vonnegut observed with the "total war" approach used during World War II. His growing interest in human behavior, along with his concerns about technology created for the mass destruction of human life, formed the basis for his writing in the following decade and beyond.

PART III

Kurt Vonnegut attended School 43 James Whitcomb Riley Elementary School in Indianapolis and often visited his hometown later in life. This photo is used with permission from Robert Weide ©Wyaduck Prods. Photog. C. Minnick

Chapter Three

Player Piano and a Trustworthy Prophet or Sharp-Eyed Satirist

In 1947, Vonnegut had gained the wisdom of one much older than his 25 years, borne of a variety of experiences: his mother's sudden death, his horrific war years, his stint as a cub reporter for Chicago's

City News Bureau. In May of that year, Vonnegut and Jane became parents of their son, Mark, and weighed opportunities in a number of cities. After consulting with his brother, Bernard, who worked as a scientist for General Electric (GE) in Schenectady, New York, Vonnegut accepted a position in the public relations department there. Bernard, designated an atmospheric chemist, discovered that infusing a chemical in the clouds could produce snow and rain. Vonnegut's experience at GE exacerbated his fears about technology. Vonnegut feared the atom bomb, fostering a concern that his country's fascination with science would lead to global destruction. His later writing demonstrated his unease with tampering with Mother Nature.

Two weeks into his job at GE in Fall of 1947, Vonnegut wrote to his father:

> I like my job. I'm not sorry that I took it, for it's better than I expected. It has an agreeable dignity to it and demands of me a certain craftmanship in which I can take pride. That, you'll agree, is important. Moreover, I'm earning, for the first time, enough to support my wife and child. And I'll have the will and time and energy to write what I please when my work is done. . ..[1]

By 1950, however, Vonnegut had grown to dislike his work at GE. He found science to be fascinating but he also feared what it would do to the planet or to American jobs and the feelings of self-worth, the sense of purpose that goes along with having a job. One day while walking through the GE plant, Vonnegut sparked the idea for his first novel, *Player Piano*.

He wrote to a friend, "It's a terrible job, so writing stories for a living is a very attractive notion. It's possible that I'll be able to make the grade in the next year. God, I sure hope so. In which case, I will, of course, write a novel about GE. It'd be about 20th Century Man, proving that he is happy – and that the glum people, like us, are a pathetic and noisy minority who write."[2]

Vonnegut boldly began *Player Piano* with a tribute to Julius Caesar's quote from *The Gallic Wars*: "All Gaul is divided into three parts, one of which the Belgae inhabit, the Aquaitani another, those who in their own language are called Celts, in our Gauls, the third." Vonnegut's opening sequence describes where the elite managers and engineers of his fictitious GE called Ilium Works lived, where the machines "live," and Homestead, where "almost all of the people live." The masses did not pass the intelligence tests that qualified individuals to attend college and obtain advanced degrees, which was the mark of success among the elite in the society he describes. Caesar wrote his book circa 46 BCE. Vonnegut's reference to Caesar's work, 2000 years later, demonstrates the timelessness, the similarity across the ages of the struggles of people in society.

Caesar's book was political propaganda. Vonnegut's book promulgated a different sort of propaganda, an anti-propaganda propaganda, with a nod to Jean Paul Sartre, who believed stories could spark social change and the writing of them was important, whether or not the actual change occurs.

Player Piano offers an interpretation of postwar industrial and corporate life featuring a common theme in science-fiction writing of the time – life after an imagined World War III. With this setting as his backdrop, Vonnegut introduced conflict including person versus technology, person versus person, and person versus society. Vonnegut's discontent with the role technology plays in society is a thread throughout his novels such as *Cat's Cradle* and *Sirens of Titan* as well as short story titles in *Welcome to the Monkey House*, speeches, and letters.

The opening page of *Player Piano* introduces the reader to the protagonist, Dr. Paul Proteus – and his cat. The cat is cast as a symbol of life, nature, instinct, the wild, perhaps even physical pleasure. The cat is kept around to be a mouser at the Ilium Works. Vonnegut has no choice but to have the electric fence kill off the cat as the machines figuratively suck the life blood out of all living things.

Proteus is named after two individuals: a sea god in Greek mythology who could change his form and nature and an electrical engineer named Charles Proteus Steinmetz, who worked for GE in its early days and was dubbed "The Engineering Wizard of Schenectady." At only 35, Proteus of *Player Piano* served as manager of Ilium Works. He had received a solid education but mostly benefited from having the last name, Proteus. His father had also risen in the ranks to lead Ilium Works before going on to more prestigious posts, including the role of his lifetime – second only to the president – the nation's first National Industrial, Commercial, Communications, Foodstuffs, and Resources Director.

Proteus's wife, Anita, is beautiful but she lacks passion for anything other than acting the wife of Proteus. We find out early that she claimed to be pregnant, perhaps to compel him to marry her. She turned out to be barren, a painful reality for Proteus, but not something he and Anita ever discuss. Proteus feels cheated out of the privilege to raise children but still tries to be what he thinks is a good husband. Anita sees herself as a good wife for much of the novel, doing her duty to help him obtain promotions in spite of his lack of ambition. The tension between Proteus and Anita grows with each chapter, as Anita is seen as demanding and solely focused on social and economic comparison with others and ladder-climbing through her husband's position. She is seen as petty with a shallow existence, a product of the postwar gender roles that American society created in an effort to return women to the home so that men could go back to the jobs that women had been filling during the war.[3] Proteus declares that Anita is "artistic" and yet there is no evidence that she creates anything. She is from "Homestead" yet she never goes back to her people to visit them, and they never visit her. Anita is ashamed of her past and tries to morph Proteus into whatever it takes to keep her in the upper echelons of the social order. She dodges each opportunity to fully love Proteus. She eventually claims to be in love with Shepherd, Proteus's would-be arch nemesis, if Proteus could have mustered the energy to care enough about Shepherd to even have an arch nemesis.

Proteus becomes dispassionate about his job, unlike Shepherd and many of the scientists and engineers who bought into the corporate culture at the corporate headquarters compound. Like the Greek mythological character of the same name who changes shapes, Proteus of *Player Piano* figuratively changes shape. He lives in the nice part of town with the engineers but goes to Anita's old stomping grounds, Homestead, where the underemployed people live. No one is striving in this society because the government ensures all are fed. Referred to as the "Reeks and Wrecks," which was slang for a mocking description of the Reconstruction and Reclamation Corps, the individuals in Homestead are mostly those considered to be unskilled since machines took their jobs and they have no formal education. They are equal only to those who served the system through military service.

Proteus is an innocent. He is the personification of the harsh realization of the cheapening of human life. While Proteus, like his namesake of Greek mythology who could change shapes, can transform himself into what he needs to be to please others, the genius in the book is the character made out as a jokester, the Shah of Bratpuhr, who was visiting in part because the State Department and others were attempting to impress him and influence him toward bringing automation to his followers. The Shah's wisdom is often delivered in a brief, scathing way, with a smile and a laugh. For example, he refers to the masses as *takaru*, which translates as "slaves" in his language. When the State Department guide, Dr. Ewing J. Halyard, attempts to correct the Shah with explanations and repeated use of the term *citizen,* the Shah continues to refer to the masses as *takaru*. The Shah is not swayed by explanations from American dignitaries regarding how happy they claim the underemployed people to be. The Shah also takes shots at communism and capitalism in his comments, further exasperating Halyard.

Vonnegut began his second chapter with a description of the Shah:

> The Shah of Bratpuhr, spiritual leader of 6,000,000 members of the Kol-houri sect, wizened and wise and dark as cocoa, encrusted with gold brocade and constellations of twinkling gems, sank deep into the royal-blue cushions of the limousine – like a priceless brooch in its gift box.[4]

Vonnegut carefully chose his words through painstaking editing. What conclusions can be drawn from the adjectives Vonnegut used to describe the character he considered to be a genius? Vonnegut uses *wizened* to vest the Shah with physical signs of having lived a long time. The Shah is also *wise*. Vonnegut intentionally separated how long a person has lived from *wisdom*. Vonnegut showed concern for prejudice and discrimination on the basis of age here and throughout his writing, often highlighting societal ageism of the elderly and children. The Shah's skin is "as dark as the color of *cocoa*," not white European as was Vonnegut's. Vonnegut was not valuing one ethnic group over another in this context. He was saying that genius can be found in all cultures and all ethnic groups, as he had learned through his study of anthropology, history, and life experience. Finally, Vonnegut focused on the dress with which the Shah was *encrusted*. Vonnegut celebrated the Shah's colorful, unique clothing – fit for someone majestic. Vonnegut's analogy compares the Shah in the limousine with royal-blue cushions compared to a brooch in its giftbox lined with blue velvet. Like the broach, the Shah and his outfit were priceless.

The most important function of the character of the Shah of Bratpuhr was to provide Vonnegut with an opportunity to address social commentary from an outsider's perspective, often the best way to observe phenomena one cannot appreciate from within. The Shah serves this purpose and delivers his commentary with humor.

The Shah was introduced to EPICAC, the supercomputer that determines nearly everything for everyone – their ability to work different jobs, the grand plan for running all aspects of society, right down to the specifications of nearly every physical object that exists in the synthetic world. EPICAC is assumed to be an abbreviation, but Vonnegut didn't spell it out in the book. EPICAC is another product of Vonnegut's unique imagination borrowed from the first real computer unveiled in 1946: ENIAC, the Electronic Numerical Integrator and Computer. EPICAC is a play on words. A commonly used medicine at the time called Ipecac aided people in the ability to vomit, for instance, if they needed to rid their stomachs of something poisonous. EPICAC also appears in a Vonnegut story of the same title published in 1950.

The Shah posed to EPICAC, "What are people for?" When the computer cannot answer that question, the Shah saw automation as a false God. The Shah realizes that EPICAC controls everyone's destiny, putting an end to individual free will in this dystopian future.

Vonnegut advanced to a high position at GE, publicist, in spite of the fact that he did not have a college degree from the many schools he attended (Butler, Cornell, University of Chicago, and the various universities he attended as part of Army training). Most GE executives had advanced degrees. He addressed this through the characters living in Homestead. Vonnegut highlighted the absurdity in American society of overvaluing doctoral degrees over real-life practical application.

A key character in the novel is Proteus's unfulfilling father-figure, Kroner, one of the elder statesmen of the Ilium Works. He was a close friend of Proteus's father, with whom Proteus had a respectful but unsatisfactory relationship. Vonnegut wrote:

> Kroner, in fact, had a poor record as an engineer and had surprised Paul from time to time with his ignorance of misunderstanding of technical matters; but he had the priceless quality of believing in the system, and of making others believe in it, too, and do as they were told.[5]

The character Ed Finnerty, on the other hand, is someone Proteus fully respects, despite his slovenly appearance. Proteus values Finnerty's mind, his independence, his subversiveness despite his advanced degree, beholden to none after pulling himself up from humble beginnings to achieve high positions. One of Finnerty's great lines of the book is a Vonnegut fan favorite: "Out on the edge you see all kinds of things you can't see from the center."[6] When Finnerty plays a player piano in Homestead, Proteus has a moment of clarity. He can no longer serve as a cog in a wheel. He does not want to support a system that replaces jobs for people with jobs for machines.

Vonnegut's feelings about the invention of the player piano were conflicted – the wonder of it in contrast with his recognition of the damage it could do to individual livelihood – present a thoughtful title for the book. Finnerty served as a counterpoint to Kroner, both of whom had a modicum of control over Proteus for opposite reasons. Near the end of the book, Proteus saw he was being used as a pawn to both those in control and to the opposition that attempted to overthrow the machines in charge. Proteus was asked by Kroner to be a double agent – to infiltrate the Ghost Shirt Society, a cabal organized to overthrow the machines, but Proteus decides in that moment to resign and take up with Finnerty and the other rebels. Vonnegut foreshadows the climax with the quote

"How about 'After us the deluge,'" referencing a statement from Louis XV prior to the French Revolution. But in *Player Piano*, the revolution is not against an aristocracy, it is a revolution against machines and the advanced degree-holders who idolize the machines. Vonnegut lists dozens of machines including Checker Charley, the electronic checkers-playing device that malfunctioned when Proteus was forced to challenge the machine to a game of checkers. The title "character," the player piano, has a ghost in the machine, making it seem once human. A memorable Orange-O drink machine and the wildly absurd but comical story of a barber robot round out the outlandish and entertaining descriptions of machines.

A meaningful exchange between Proteus and his "secretary" Katharine Finch helps capture the message Vonnegut conveys with this book. Finch is the only woman who works at Ilium Works. Although her administrative skills were pedestrian, she serves as a "stand in" for Proteus when he is unavailable. While Proteus writes about the First and Second Industrial Revolutions, it is Finch who suggests to Proteus there might be a Third Industrial Revolution. Proteus reflected, "A third one, eh? In a way, I guess the third one's been going on for some time, if you mean thinking machines. That would be the third revolution, I guess —machines that devaluate human thinking."[7]

Finch adds, "First the muscle work, then the routine work, then, maybe, the real brainwork." Proteus laments, "I hope I'm not around long enough to see that final step."[8]

Proteus's existential crisis leads him to recognize that he can choose to be a passive observer or an active leader in taking back society for the people. After the revolution fails and Proteus is standing tall in the courtroom, he claims responsibility for the entirety of the revolution – a movement that he came to quite late in the process. Members of the Ghost Shirt Society were subversives, and the government and corporate leaders reacted to Proteus and these rebels similarly to the 1950s McCarthy anti-communism approach that Vonnegut witnessed when he was writing the story. As insidious as was McCarthy's approach, it was different from the actual Ghost Dance Movement that faced its conclusion at the "Massacre of Wounded Knee" in 1890, when 300 indigenous peoples were shot to death by members of the US Cavalry while camped out on Wounded Knee Creek. Vonnegut, sympathetic to their plight, refers to indigenous peoples with compassion and respect in the book.

Vonnegut disguised aspects of *Player Piano* in deference to his brother, Bernard, who remained employed at GE. Vonnegut modified details when he described the corporate brainwashing that took place not just at GE but at many multinational corporations through a play performed at an annual Ilium Works retreat that Proteus is expected to attend at an island called "The Meadows." The Meadows was created to provide an environment for the engineers and managers of Ilium Works to get to know one another in the spirit of networking and partly to fuel the corporate propaganda machine and cement employee loyalty by making their work seem critical to society. The play is based on actual events created by General Electric to pump up employees. The play imagined by Vonnegut for *Player Piano* features, among other characters, John Averageman who speaks of his 80 percent drop in pay since he went from being a regular worker prior to the war to his postwar position among the Reeks and Wrecks. He says, "...The average man is just nothing anymore."[9] But after being convinced by fast-talking, slick "Young Engineer," John Averageman decides that his big-screened TV does, indeed, make him better off than famous leaders like Henry VIII, Julius Caesar, Charlemagne, and Napoleon. Vonnegut voiced his concern in 1952 that big-screen TVs would distract people from real living. In the play, which was written by a character from Indiana, Vonnegut mocked corporate culture while giving a tip of the hat to the working stiff and the soldier.

Vonnegut was a master of revealing absurdity, as evidenced by the ending of *Player Piano*, where he depicts the futility of giving a damn as the revolutionaries, those set to destroy the machines, would go on to create the exact same environment they went to such great lengths to destroy. Vonnegut implored the reader to think, determine who the revolution is serving, and decide whether they are simply pawns for another king.

Like Proteus, Vonnegut left GE, his own Ilium Works, in January 1951. Proteus knew the importance of buying a farmhouse to reconnect with living a simpler, less-mechanized life. Vonnegut and Jane bought their own farmhouse later in the year in West Barnstable, Massachusetts. In that pivotal year, *Player Piano* was published, and Vonnegut learned he had something important to say and that people were eager to listen to this new, fresh voice from Indiana.

In 1970, twenty years after writing *Player Piano*, Vonnegut delivered his first of many graduation speeches at Bennington College, Vermont. He said:

> It has been said many times that man's knowledge of himself has been left far behind by his understanding of technology, and that we can have peace and plenty and justice only when man's knowledge of himself catches up. This is not true. Some people hope for great discoveries in the social sciences, social equivalents of $F = ma$ and $E = mc^2$, and so on. Others think we have to evolve, to become better monkeys with bigger brains. We don't need more information. We don't need bigger brains. All that is required is that we become less selfish than we are.[10]

In *Player Piano*, Vonnegut expressed the need for people to take personal responsibility for their choices. He simultaneously encouraged exercising free will over conformity or divine authority while also making it clear that free will is nearly impossible for most people to benefit from due to governmental authority, but for Vonnegut, life is also a series of accidents. Vonnegut expressed with this story a sense of heavy disappointment in human beings for not giving other human beings what he believed was most important in life: opportunities to show self-worth through labor or creativity, physical affection in love relationships, attention, unconditional love, spending quality time with people more often than with technology – all or any of which lead to a sense of feeling alive.

Vonnegut gave his books letter grades from A through F. He gave *Player Piano* a B. A *New York Times* book critic concluded his review with this: "Whether he is a trustworthy prophet or not, Mr. Vonnegut is a sharp-eyed satirist."[11]

Chapter Four

"Harrison Bergeron": A Twist on David and Goliath for the Civil Rights Era

One is hard-pressed to find a short story in American literature more misunderstood than "Harrison Bergeron," a short story that continues to remain as relevant and popular as when it was released. Those who misinterpret "Harrison Bergeron" believe it serves as an example of why equality is not an acceptable concept. Many individuals and organizations have misappropriated the story for their own political purposes, incorrectly suggesting that Vonnegut sees equality as a bad thing.

This misinterpretation, the absurdity of it, was a disappointment to Vonnegut. Read as Vonnegut intended, "Harrison Bergeron" attempts to mock those who are afraid of people different from themselves, those who fear equality. This story was written as a satire.

Vonnegut was not strictly a satirist, but he occasionally used satire as a means to spotlight the absurd. Vonnegut highlights two concepts with this story: his concern with governmental overreach and abuse, which could result in revolutions, and his mockery of those who feared the developing efforts to create Civil Rights legislation. Vonnegut's point with this story is that citizens should endeavor to make things better.

"Harrison Bergeron" was published by Mystery House in *The Maga-zine of Fantasy and Science Fiction* in 1961, one of the leading maga-zines in this field at the time. It appeared in *National Review* in 1965 and reappeared in 1968 in the bound collection *Welcome to the Monkey House*, published by Delacorte. That collection features sci-fi storylines and other adventures, nearly all of which have a moral that relates to the need for people to treat others with common decency. Govern-ment overreach and abuse could be found in American culture and politics during this period as evidenced by governmental propaganda spread through television and other avenues promoting conservative values, Cold-War era surveillance and McCarthyism, and efforts by seg-regationists to maintain a racist system.

The story presents a dystopian future where the concept of equal-ity has been twisted and demeaned, creating a frightening reality. The year is 2081, and Vonnegut's future imagines a governing system that has control over citizens' bodies and thoughts. On the first page, we meet a pleasant couple, George and Hazel Bergeron, and the Handi-capper General, Diana Moon Glampers. She is the evil leader at the helm of a repressive, conformist society, along with her henchmen who ensure that no one is better than anyone else. Vonnegut typi-cally doesn't have a "bad guy" in his stories. He wrote in a later work, *Slaughterhouse-Five*, about his graduate school experience: "Another thing they taught was that no one was ridiculous or bad or disgust-ing. Shortly before my father died, he said to me, 'You know – you never wrote a story with a villain in it.' I told him that was one of the things I learned in college after the war."[1] Vonnegut's father died in 1957. Diana Moon Glampers may be the only villain in his oeuvre. It may be intentional or coincidental that he introduced a villain after his father died.

One act demonstrating Glampers as a villain occurs when she sends agents to forcibly remove from the Bergerons' home their 14-year-old son Harrison, presumably because he is subversive. Vonnegut does not pause here to talk about young Harrison, but it's worth further exploration as governmental overreach prohibits parents from the right and obligation to assume responsibility over their children. While there is no description of this horrific day, Vonnegut conveys a frightening reality of a totalitarian government that could force seemingly loving parents to comply with the Handicapper General's orders. Later in the story, Harrison, as a 14-year-old boy, becomes a fugitive and a revolutionist. Harrison was 7 feet tall with incredible strength and will.

In Vonnegut's collection of short stories, there are multiple tales of misunderstood or underappreciated boys. Through his adult life, Vonnegut straddled being a grown-up, dealing with challenging experiences and difficult decision-making while also being an unapologetic boy. Some of his most beloved stories are sensitive to boys coming of age. Vonnegut viewed his childhood as perhaps the very best period of his life. In 2005, at age 83, Vonnegut said to a *Toronto Globe* reporter: "Where is home? I've wondered where home is, and I realized, it's not Mars or someplace like that, it's Indianapolis when I was nine years old. I had a brother and a sister, a cat and a dog, and a mother and a father and uncles and aunts. And there's no way I can get there again."[2]

Vonnegut's boy characters, lovable one and all, end up facing harsh realities that cause them to have to grow up fast – the youngest is Karl Heinz, a.k.a. "Joe Louis" a 6-year-old black orphan in Germany in the short story "D.P." in the *Welcome to the Monkey House* collection. The oldest was Billy Pilgrim at age 21 when he is captured by the Nazis in *Slaughterhouse-Five*.

Harrison Bergeron, while feistier than other boy characters in Vonnegut's work, is hailed as a boy who took on a tyrant – a David versus Goliath scenario – except in this scenario, the child is a large physical specimen yet with a boy's mind and heart. Harrison is the hero of the story but Vonnegut doesn't make it quite that easy. Harrison is not a hero in the way some films and books portray a hero: flawless, the perfect person, the perfect spouse, parent, or citizen. Harrison is a hero who some Vonnegut scholars consider flawed because he does not hide his ambition, passion, or rage.

While the scenes with Harrison comprise the action of the story, most of the story unfolds as George and Hazel are watching television in their home, the common activity in this society. This is a government-forced distraction, a popular refrain in 1950s and 1960s science fiction, where people moved from a society of social gathering to a society where people locked themselves away each night to watch the blue TV screen, often fearing those outside their homes.

In the Bergeron home, George is watching TV with Hazel as ballerinas on the screen are saddled with heavy weights and ugly masks to cause them to be "equal" to or less graceful and less attractive than any individuals who don a tutu. They are mediocre, a characteristic Vonnegut was raised to believe was unacceptable. George has revolutionary thoughts as he is watching the ballet that ballerinas shouldn't be saddled with weights and masks. Each time he has a critical thought of the government's bizarre approach to equality, the government radio terrifies him and causes his thoughts to pacify or simply disappear altogether. The government uses transmitters – "a little mental handicap radio" – to make sounds that prevent George, with his above-average intelligence, from thinking linear thoughts beyond a few seconds. The sound is so alarming that it leads to panic, causing George and all of those encumbered with this government-imposed device to quickly change their thoughts and lose their memory of them.

The authoritarian reach on Hazel is not a radio transmitter but is simply the addictive, State-controlled programming that causes her to be fixated with the screen. The story begins as Hazel is crying because of something she saw on television, but she doesn't know why she is crying. She doesn't remember what she saw only moments before. Hazel has been reeducated to believe the State has everyone's best interests at heart, yet she suggests that George could remove heavy weights on his neck that had been placed on him to further handicap him. George chooses not to take the risk of setting down his heavy weights even though the risk may be minimal as there is no advanced surveillance within their household.

An announcement of a special report interrupted the ballet. Harrison had escaped from jail, intruded on the televised ballet performance, declared himself to be emperor, and requested a ballerina drop her handicaps and mask and join him as empress.

Harrison and others perhaps assume that the dancers are attractive because of their especially hideous masks, but Harrison is not interested in mere looks. He is interested in bravery and loyalty. He is interested in the person who will put her life at risk for freedom and for his love. A particular ballerina who removed her mask and was described as "blindingly beautiful" didn't hesitate to join Harrison. Vonnegut wrote: "Not only were the laws of the land abandoned, but the law of gravity and the laws of motion as well."[3] Harrison and his empress ascended. Vonnegut, a life-long romantic, put the reader in the mind of a 14-year-old boy who had been in jail and was now experiencing what might be his first kiss, ". . . neutralizing gravity with love and pure will. . . they kissed each other for a long, long time."[4]

> It was then that Diana Moon Glampers, the Handicapper General, came into the studio with a double-barreled ten-gauge shotgun. She fired twice, and the Emperor and the Empress were dead before they hit the floor.[5]

Use of a ten-gauge shotgun was low tech for a sci-fi story, considering these guns were first used in the United States in the late 1800s. With exceptionally intelligent individuals being dulled by the government transmitters, there may have been no ability to imagine and create new technology in Vonnegut's created future. Diana Moon Glampers could have jailed Harrison and the ballerina, but instead she chose a method of swift deterrence. She made an example of them. The confusion for many with this story may result from what Vonnegut didn't say rather than what he did say.

At some point while the two were watching television, George went to the kitchen momentarily and returned to find Hazel had been crying. She didn't know why she had been crying. The reader knew she cried because she witnessed the TV reportage of her son Harrison's murder by the Handicapper General along with the murder of a ballerina.

Television news, newspapers, and magazine headlines leading up to the time during which Vonnegut wrote this story often focused on escalating violence against African Americans, as well as violence in other areas of the world from Vietnam to Algeria.

While legislation related to Americans with disabilities did not come until many years after Civil Rights Legislation for minorities and women, it is impossible to place "Harrison Bergeron" in its proper framework without understanding the historical backdrop during which it was written. A review of several moments in the struggle for civil rights legislation, which coincided with Vonnegut's writing, is necessary to better understand this story. This is not a complete list, but these events shed light:

1948: President Harry Truman ended segregation in the military.

1954: A Supreme Court case, *Brown v. Board of Education*, ended racial segregation in public schools.

1955: 14-year-old Emmett Till was murdered in Mississippi for "flirting with a white woman."

1955: Rosa Parks refused to move from her bus seat, leading to the Montgomery bus boycott.

1957: Black leaders united in ending segregation and racial discrimination met to organize nonviolent protests.

1957: President Dwight Eisenhower sent federal troops to Arkansas to support the integration of nine black students into Little Rock High School.

1960: The first "sit-in" occurred in North Carolina when four black college students refused to leave a lunch counter without being served. George Wallace, who had failed at his attempt to run for the position of Alabama governor, was mounting a new campaign backed by the Ku Klux Klan. Segregationists like Wallace were doubling down to prevent continued efforts to pass civil rights legislation.

1961: "Harrison Bergeron" was published in October.

White segregationists saw the Civil Rights Movement as a threat to their own rights. Some imagined other individuals to be as hate-filled as they were and feared their own torturous methods would be turned back on to them. They lobbied politicians to maintain the same racist system. In Harrison Bergeron, the only person who seemed frightened of Harrison or of the ballerinas or those with advanced critical thinking skills was the Handicapper General. Vonnegut provides an example of how the *absence* of difference causes the malfunctions in this dystopian society.

Harrison is a product of his totalitarian environment. He observed from an authoritarian system how to be dictatorial. It's unsurprising that he would demand to assume the role of emperor. Harrison practiced acts of free will when he escaped, commandeered television attention, and asked a dancer to unmask and be his Empress. He did not demand dancers unmask and then choose among them. He was looking for someone to voluntarily practice free will, but he also was not suggesting he would free everyone from bondage.

Some scholars say readers should avoid the trap of thinking Vonnegut was talking about US/Soviet relations with this story. However, the thought of comparison with a hegemonic, totalitarian regime is tempting. Vonnegut understood regime change and revolutions based on his education as well as his war experience and his observation of Germany as it moved from a fascist country to a half-communist/half-democratic country. He understood communist overreach. Dresden, in particular, was in Communist East Germany. He also despised the US government's efforts to weed out communism in America, the melting pot. Vonnegut valued democracy, dialogue, and cooperation. He should not be placed in a category of communist, capitalist, socialist, or any other political party. He was none of them and all of them.

Vonnegut spoke of the ruthlessness with which authoritarians will prevent social change. Unsuccessful in protecting his son from Diana Moon Glampers, George Bergeron doesn't remove his handicaps, despite the fact that there is no known surveillance system inside his home, because he has given up. Vonnegut's message is always: Don't give up.

Near the end of his life, Vonnegut expressed concern that "Harrison Bergeron" had been misinterpreted by some readers. In one case in 2005, where attorneys for a school system in Kansas said: "The story of Harrison Bergeron shows that a world of forced equality would be a nightmare, so unequal funding of public schools is OK,"[6] Vonnegut's reply stated that the attorneys may have misinterpreted the story. Vonnegut told the newspaper *Lawrence Journal-World*, "It's about intelligence and talent, and wealth is not a demonstration of either one." He added, "Kansas is apparently handicapping schoolchildren, no matter how gifted and talented, with lousy educations if their parents are poor."[7]

Chapter Five

Slaughterhouse-Five and a New Kind of Patriot

I n early 1969, Vonnegut had become highly regarded as a writer but was not yet a household name. Not only had he sold several hundred thousand copies of his early books but in 1965 he also had worked as a professor at the Iowa Writers Workshop, a renowned literary educational experience that produced alumni such as Flannery O'Connor and Raymond Carver, who completed his studies just one year prior to Vonnegut's arrival.

While students at Iowa were engaged with their projects, they and nearly all Americans were preoccupied with the Vietnam War. By 1969, the American death toll had run into the tens of thousands. Vonnegut couldn't have picked a better time to release an antiwar book. *Slaughterhouse-Five* is one of the most important antiwar books ever written. Vonnegut said, "And what I saw, what I had to report, made war look so ugly. You know, the truth can be really powerful stuff."[1] The timing of the novel's release was not intentional. It was *lucky*. It had taken Vonnegut more than twenty years and countless discarded draft pages as well as a return to Dresden to hone this story to his satisfaction.

The Epigraph in *Slaughterhouse-Five* quotes the Christmas song "Away in a Manger":

The cattle are lowing,

The baby awakes.

But the little Lord Jesus

No crying he makes.[2]

This reference to Jesus is analogous to Billy Pilgrim, the story's protagonist, a defenseless person launched into a cruel world, silently bearing his experience. Vonnegut writes later in the book: "Billy cried very little, though he often saw things worth crying about, and in that respect, at least, he resembled the Christ of the carol."[3]

The epigraph transitions the reader into the novel's first chapter, which features Vonnegut as blended author and narrator in first-person narrative. Rather than providing an explanation for his thought process in an introduction, Vonnegut took this unusual approach to Chapter One because he thought the insights and historical background were critical to the story. This approach is one reason *Slaughterhouse-Five* is groundbreaking. Vonnegut as author/narrator and Pilgrim, the protagonist, had different but overlapping experiences that Vonnegut demonstrates as relevant to contemporary issues of the time of the book's release. Vonnegut as narrator introduces his belief that free will is an illusion, and added that he intended to write an antiwar book to which an acquaintance of his, Harrison Starr, said, "Why don't you write an anti-*glacier* book instead?" Vonnegut says: "What he meant, of course, was that there would always be wars, that they were as easy to stop as glaciers. I believe that, too. And even if wars didn't keep coming like glaciers, there would still be plain old death."[4]

Pilgrim, like Vonnegut as narrator, is captured by the Nazis during the Battle of the Bulge in 1944. The Nazis force march their captives sixty miles in the snow to board a train bound for, among other places, a prison-of-war (POW) camp in a building used as a pig slaughterhouse in Dresden, Germany. The transport experience is its own separate nightmare. Men are crammed into boxcars that sit on the tracks for two days without moving, and they must take a creative approach to excretion and sustenance. The Royal Air Force strafed the box cars enroute to Dresden, mistakenly thinking they bore German soldiers or war materiel for Germany's front. Many of Pilgrim's comrades in arms perished in the boxcar deathtrap. Upon arrival in Dresden, they experience moments of fellowship but mostly deprivation and cruelty. When the Allies firebomb Dresden, Pilgrim survives because he is underground, but the residents and transients on the surface succumb to smoke inhalation, fire, or collapsed buildings.

During his time in Dresden, Pilgrim is known to his fellow POWs, but he is essentially alone. His enemies, from the Nazis to fellow POWs, exacerbate his loneliness. The captives meet American traitor Howard Campbell, who became a Nazi. They meet Paul Lazzaro, an American fellow POW who brags about committing vengeance against anyone who wrongs him, directly or indirectly. Lazzaro vows to have Pilgrim killed because he blames Pilgrim's lack of boots and fortitude for the death of his only friend, a POW named Roland Weary, an unlikable character to all but Lazzaro. Pilgrim believes that Lazzaro will kill him out of revenge for Weary's death from gangrene. Pilgrim is prescient.

When Pilgrim returns from the war, he studies to be an optometrist, marries, and raises a family: a boy, a girl, and a dog. Pilgrim suffers from what some characterize as post-traumatic stress disorder (PTSD). In his damaged mental state, he travels across time and space to the planet Tralfamadore, where Tralfamadorians place him in a cage with a beautiful woman, Montana Wildhack. The captives fall madly in love, to the delight of the Tralfamadorians, who watch their behaviors – including procreation and breastfeeding. The Tralfamadorians share with Pilgrim insightful contrasts between life on Earth and Tralfama-dore. Pilgrim's thoughts drift back and forth between his past, pre-sent, and future as part of his time travel, which Vonnegut refers to as being "unstuck in time." Upon returning to the present from a time-travel trip, Pilgrim survives a plane crash, but his wife dies of carbon monoxide poisoning on the way to the hospital to see Pilgrim after she gets into a car accident. Pilgrim convalesces in a nursing home. Following more time travel, Pilgrim delivers a lecture to an audience in Chicago when he is shot to death, as promised by Lazarro. Pilgrim is not dismayed during his last moments of life because he expects this outcome. He understands time differently, as he has seen his death and other moments of his life many times. Pilgrim's death is not the end of the story. Like the story of Jesus, Vonnegut wants his character to live on in the imagination of future readers. Also, as in the first chapter where he sets the scene for the introduction of the story of Billy Pilgrim, in the final chapter, Vonnegut returns as narrator/author speaking directly to his readers about the firebombing of Dresden, as well as events that were taking place during the time he was writing the book – the murders of Robert Kennedy and Martin Luther King Jr.

Breaking down *Slaughterhouse-Five* should begin with the original title: *Slaughterhouse-Five or The Children's Crusade: A Duty Dance with Death*. The book is dedicated to Mary O'Hare and Gerhard Müller. The narrator shares that Müller was a German cab driver whom he met on his return visit to Dresden, and Mary O'Hare is the wife of his best war buddy, Bernard V. O'Hare. Mary learns Vonnegut as narrator is writing a book about the war and worries that it is going to be full of bravado and commemoration of bloodshed rather than voicing the truth that the war was devastating and was fought, she said, by "babies." Vonnegut as narrator agrees with her that the soldiers who fought in the war *were* like babies, innocent, seeing the world as it is for the first time. Vonnegut as narrator shares that this conversation with Mary O'Hare provided the perspective he needed for his approach with the book. He pledges to title the book *The Children's Crusade,* which is a reference to an event in European Christian history when German and French orphaned and otherwise deserted children, believing they were going to Palestine to fight as part of the Crusades, were instead taken from Europe and sold to slave traders in North Africa.

Vonnegut explains in Chapter One that this subtitle was borrowed from the words of Louis-Ferdinand Céline: *"No art is possible without a dance with death..."* Vonnegut added: *Time obsessed him."*[5] A biography of Celine titled *Celine and His Vision* explains that the World War I French soldier Céline became a doctor-by-day, author-by-night, and eventual antisemitic propagandist. It suggests that his writing came from a mind suffering from PTSD, which previously had been referred to as *shell shock*. Vonnegut's study of these issues is reflected in Pilgrim's behaviors.

Vonnegut introduced characters based on real people he met during his military service. For example, "poor old Edgar Derby" was shot to death for attempting to steal a teapot following the destruction of Dresden. Vonnegut's reference to "poor old Edgar Derby" throughout the book demonstrates that he believes Derby's murder to be unjust, considering his crime is minor. Vonnegut had befriended this individual, who was a well-liked man of integrity. Vonnegut was pained by his death. The absurdity of Derby's death is one of many examples of death in the story that leads to Vonnegut's larger point that war is absurd.

The character Lazzaro is based on someone Vonnegut says in the narrative really did threaten to have his personal enemies killed after the war. Vonnegut's tone comes across as disapproving when he adds that this individual stole a quart of jewels from victims of the firebombing.

In the first chapter, Vonnegut introduces the phrase "So it goes" after recalling someone's death. What is the "it" in "so it goes"? *It* is life. Some scholars say "it" is death. Both interpretations arrive at the same conclusion, which it that everyone is going to die at some point. Vonnegut repeated this phrase more than a hundred times in the book. It serves as a reminder that people are not in control of their lives, but is also a reminder to the narrator and the reader not to stay depressed about life's tragedies for too long. Vonnegut as narrator says we are not meant to look back on death because death is part of life. He focuses on the Bible story in Genesis, in which Lot's wife and others who had left Sodom had been commanded by God not to look back at the city, which was being destroyed by God.

Vonnegut writes: "And Lot's wife, of course, was told not to look back where all those people and their homes had been. But she did look back, and I love her for that, because it was so human. So she was turned into a pillar of salt. So it goes."[6]

While she is traveling with others, Lot's wife is the only one to look back – it is her home, and she had family there. Like Vonnegut, she was a witness to the destruction of a city. To Vonnegut, who believed Bible stories were not meant to be read literally but instead presented important tales of morals and ethics, this ancient wisdom was clear: *People are not supposed to look back*. While it may seem inconsistent for Vonnegut to say he loves her for looking back while simultaneously saying people are not supposed to look back, Vonnegut's point is that some amount of this type of sentimentality is important to ensure we remain humane. Too little sentimentality leads to the type of callousness and mental illness demonstrated by the Nazis. Too much sentimentality causes suffering and other mental health challenges for those unable to move forward.

Vonnegut ends Chapter One – again breaking with conventional writing – by telling the reader the first and last lines of the book. The first being, "Listen. Billy Pilgrim has become unstuck in time." The last line is: "Poo-tee-weet?"[7]

Vonnegut's personal correspondence throughout his life reveals that he used the word *listen* to start sentences that included thoughts particularly important to him. But the word also implies that readers are about to be treated to a legend, profound thought, or revelation. Vonnegut occasionally borrowed ideas from other writers in an effort both to recognize past thinkers in the world of philosophy, poetry, and literature – but also to recast their thoughts into a contemporary or differing perspective. The use of *listen* calls to mind a poem many American schoolchildren of Vonnegut's era could recite, a poem, "Paul Revere's Ride" by Henry Wadsworth Longfellow, that begins:

"Listen, my children, and you shall hear of the midnight ride of Paul Revere."[8]

The first line of *Slaughterhouse-Five* also opens with "Listen" and introduces the name of the main character: "Listen. Billy Pilgrim has become unstuck in time."

It connects the reader to time and harkens back to a story written just over 100 years earlier. "Paul Revere's Ride" features a courageous patriot, Revere, a character based on an actual soldier in the American Revolutionary War. If *Slaughterhouse-Five* is a legend, Pilgrim is the antithesis to Paul Revere. He is not full of military decorum and self-assuredness – but Vonnegut wants readers to know him as a patriot, like the thousands of soldiers who served in Vonnegut's war. "Experience taught Vonnegut that real wars rob people of their ability to act heroically."[9] Pilgrim, a young man with no self-confidence, *tries.* He serves his country by going to war to fight fascism. He is the epitome of Mary O'Hare's "baby." Vonnegut mentions the American enlisted soldiers' shoddy uniform in comparisons to the Englishmen's uniforms and those of the American military officers. Pilgrim is a stark contrast to professional refinement.

Among other things in common with "Paul Revere's Ride," *Slaughterhouse-Five* mentions birds. The last line of the book is: "Poo-tee-weet?" Longfellow wrote, "And startled the pigeons from their perch." More closely related to "poo-tee-weet," though, is Longfellow's "And the twitter of birds among the trees."

Further comparison between the two works reveals more on the concept of time, beyond the opening sentences. Longfellow carries the reader through the actions each hour as the clock strikes.

For example, Longfellow wrote, "It was twelve by the village clock when he crossed the bridge into Medford town," and, "It was one by the village clock, When he galloped into Lexington."[10]

Vonnegut's book is filled with time moving back and forth, spanning decades of Pilgrim's time travels.

Another commonality between the two works is that both serve as propaganda. "Paul Revere's Ride" is a nationalistic, prowar tribute poem aimed to excite young readers about war, its gallantry, and the townspeople sticking together for a common cause. *Slaughterhouse-Five* is an anti-nationalism, antiwar novel that aims to excite young readers about *peace* through the honest description of the horrors of war. Vonnegut accurately portrays the absurdities of military life, where sometimes there are "Lazarros" and others who shatter the concept of *esprit de corps*.

Vonnegut tells the reader he will end the book with a bird saying "poo-tee-weet?" because, he says:

> *Everything is supposed to be very quiet after a massacre, and it always is, except for the birds.*
>
> *And what do the birds say? All there is to say about a massacre, things like "Poo-tee-weet?"*[11]

The allusion to birds in a war-related creative work can also be found in a poem Vonnegut knew, "In Flanders Fields" by a World War I Canadian military officer and doctor named John McCraé. McCrae wrote the poem after speaking at the funeral of a friend and fellow soldier:

In Flanders Fields

In Flanders Fields, the poppies blow
Between the crosses, row on row,
That mark our place; and in the sky
The larks, still bravely singing, fly
Scarce heard amid the guns below.

We are the dead. Short days ago
We lived, felt dawn, saw sunset glow,
Loved and were loved, and now we lie,
In Flanders fields.

Take up our quarrel with the foe:
To you from failing hands we throw
The torch; be yours to hold it high.
If ye break faith with us who die
We shall not sleep, though poppies grow
In Flanders fields.[12]

For the sake of clarity, Vonnegut's transition from Chapter One to Chapter Two needs repeating. A the end of Chapter One, Vonnegut tells the reader that the first line of the story is "Listen. Billy Pilgrim has become unstuck in time." He then says that the last line of the book is "Poo-tee-weet?" Chapter Two begins as foretold: "Listen. Billy Pilgrim has become unstuck in time." This line begins the "legend" of Pilgrim. While many people think Billy Pilgrim *was* Vonnegut, that was not the case.

> *I am going to tell you something that's not generally known: I wrote a book called Slaughterhouse-Five and the leading character was named Billy Pilgrim. And he was, in fact, modeled after a young man from Rochester.*[13]

During the War, Vonnegut befriended Edward "Joe" Crone, a young soldier from New York. Like McCrae's writing of "In Flanders Fields" in memorial to his fellow soldier, *Slaughterhouse-Five* is a literary monument to Joe Crone and all of the soldiers and civilians who died in the war, any war, but specifically in Dresden during World War II.

Nicknamed in childhood as "Goony," Crone was a lanky and awkward "gentle soul." Crone had been an Eagle Scout and wanted to become a chaplain. He believed his duty was not to kill people but to save people and to fight fascism.

Like Vonnegut, Crone was captured in the Ardennes as part of the Battle of the Bulge. He struggled to fit in with the other prisoners. The Nazis were especially cruel to him. Like Vonnegut, Crone witnessed the destructive firebombing of Dresden and suffered the vision of burned bodies of countless children, women, pets, and other noncombatants. He could not process or accept man's cruelty and lost the will to live. He chose to stop eating. Vonnegut said Crone had the "thousand-yard stare," one outcome of post-traumatic stress in which the individual had suffered psychological trauma in a way that causes people to be unresponsive to things around them.

Crone died less than a month before Vonnegut was liberated. Years later, to Vonnegut's surprise, Crone was reinterred in Crone's hometown in Upstate New York (see Chapter Six). Vonnegut said, "Joe was deeply religious and kind of childlike. The war was utterly incomprehensible to him, as it should have been."[14]

The way in which Crone died – not the way Pilgrim died – provides insight into Vonnegut's belief that while there is free will and while life is a series of accidents, humans must still *try* – try to survive, to be happy, to improve their communities, to raise families or help raise extended family, and to make life more bearable for other people and themselves.

Just as Vonnegut used the Shah of Bratpuhr in *Player Piano* to reveal important truths, he incorporates seemingly whimsical outsiders, the Tralfamadorians from the planet Tralfamadore, in *Slaughterhouse-Five* to educate Pilgrim (and readers) about American life in comparison to life on planet Tralfamadore, including their most important idea that free will doesn't exist and their unusual view on time and the progression of life. Vonnegut writes of one Tralfamadorian theory:

> . . .when a person dies he only *appears* to die. He is still very much alive in the past, present and future, always has existed, always will exist. . . . When a Tralfamadorian sees a corpse, all he thinks is that the dead person is in bad condition in that particular moment, but that the person is just fine in plenty of other moments. Now, when I myself hear that somebody is dead, I simply shrug and say what the Tralfamadorians say about dead people, which is "So it goes."[15]

While the Tralfamadorians offer insights that are often wise, Vonnegut Scholar Thomas Marvin wrote that "attentive readers will notice the parallels between Tralfamadorian fatalism and the Nazis' outlook on life," for example, when Nazis avoided responsibility for their murder and torture of others. Marvin said the evidence for this is the answer to Billy Pilgrim's question of "Why me?" when they respond: "Vy you? Vy anyone?"[16]

Vonnegut was playful with his description of Tralfamadorians:

[They] were two feet high, and green, and shaped like plumber's friends. Their suction cups were on the ground, and their shafts, which were extremely flexible, usually pointed to the sky. At the top of the shaft was a little hand with a green eye in its palm. The creatures were friendly, and they could see in four dimensions. They pitied Earthlings for being able to see only three. They had many wonderful things to teach Earthlings, especially about time.[17]

Pilgrim's time on Tralfamadore has been compared with John Milton's *Paradise Lost*, an epic poem that places the Bible story of Adam, Eve, and the Garden of Eden in domestic scene. Vonnegut describes a scene in which Pilgrim is preoccupied with thoughts of Adam and Eve during the war:

"But, lying on the black ice there, Billy stared into the patina of the corporal's boots, saw Adam and Eve in the golden depths. They were naked. They were so innocent, so vulnerable, so eager to behave decently. Billy Pilgrim loved them."[18]

In one of Pilgrim's postwar PTSD-inspired time travels, Eve is represented as the character Montana Wildhack. Wildhack had been an erotic actress – a porn star. Billy adores her. They share their version of Eden on Tralfamadore. Their relationship is kind and loving. They learn to trust each other and enjoy a wonderful physical relationship. The unconditional love that Paul Proteus yearned for in *Player Piano* and Harrison Bergeron demanded in Vonnegut's short story of the same title was fully developed in *Slaughterhouse-Five* as an ideal (seemingly unrealistic) unconditional love between Pilgrim and Wildhack in his imaginary world on Tralfamadore. Though many see unconditional love beyond love for one's children as unrealistic, Vonnegut believed it was achievable. For Vonnegut, unconditional love did not mean unconditional tolerance of all behavior. Vonnegut's correspondence suggested that for him, unconditional love meant the absence of cruelty and in a romantic relationship, was acceptance and endless affection – an *uncritical* love as evidenced by Pilgrim who, for the first time in his life, was not ashamed of his body. The ever-observing Tralfamadorians assume Pilgrim is a perfect human specimen so he, for once, feels handsome, viral, beautiful. Beyond the physical relationship between Wildhack and Pilgrim, their friendship and conversation make their relationship strong, and Pilgrim finally feels safe enough to tell Wildhack the story of what happened in Dresden, the most painful experience of his life.

Slaughterhouse-Five has been banned in schools because of the sexual relationship between Wildhack and Pilgrim. The book has also been attacked by fundamentalist Christians and atheists alike because of its references to Jesus. Lest readers mistake Vonnegut for a Christian (although he celebrated Christian holidays with his family and Jewish holidays with his Jewish friends), long-time friend and best-selling author Dan Wakefield shared his perspective:

> There seems to be something between Jesus and Kurt Vonnegut – though it certainly is not a belief in his divinity (Vonnegut registers frustration that "they had to make him a God"), but an admiration, a fascination, and a kind of kinship with the man he called "my wild and loving brother". . .[19]

Vonnegut features the Serenity Prayer in the final chapter of the book. He also uses the final chapter to provide gruesome details of the firebombing of Dresden and the aftermath, including the mass burials, unjust murder of poor old Edgar Derby, and contemporary crises of the day.

Marvin wrote, "It is also a book about America in the 1960s. Vonnegut portrays a nation that has betrayed its founding principles of democracy, freedom, justice, and opportunity for all. By calling for a return to these principles, Vonnegut engaged the conscience of a generation and wrote a novel that is widely regarded as an American classic."[20]

In March 1969, a *New York Times* reviewer wrote: "Mr. Vonnegut pronounces his book a failure 'because there is nothing intelligent to say about a massacre.' He's wrong and he knows it."[21]

The reviewer went on to say:

"It sounds crazy. It sounds like a fantastic last-ditch effort to make sense of a lunatic universe. But there is so much more to this book. It is very tough and very funny; it is sad and delightful; and it works. But it is also very Vonnegut, which means you'll either love it or push it back in the science-fiction corner."[22]

After twenty years of revising manuscripts, Seymour Lawrence, a Dell Publishing editor, offered to purchase *Slaughterhouse-Five*, along with Vonnegut's next two novels, for a "shocking" amount of money to which Vonnegut replied, "You're out of your mind. You'll never make that back."[23] Between Dell and later publishers, millions of copies of *Slaughterhouse-Five* have sold in forty-one languages. The book is read in schools around the globe. It inspires the work of artists, musicians, and filmmakers. It is read by foot soldiers and those of the highest ranks at war colleges. It successfully serves as propaganda for peace, Vonnegut's greatest achievement.

PART IV

Kurt Vonnegut created a paper airplane during a visit to Indianapolis with friend and documentarian Robert Weide. This photo is used with permission from Robert Weide ©whyaduck Prods. Photog. C. Minnick

PART IV

Chapter Six
The True Measure of a Man

Following the success of *Slaughterhouse-Five*, Vonnegut was in high demand for interviews, graduation speeches, new book contracts, or simply, his time. He and Jane had suffered through a host of challenges – including the painful period when Vonnegut's sister and her husband died, leaving three of their four children in the care of the Vonneguts. While the children grew up, finished high school, and entered college, Vonnegut continued to write. Though Jane spent the early years praising his work and making suggestions, in later years, their conversations about his writing were less positive or productive.

"My mother gave him a lot of criticism and then they'd have these terrible fights. He wanted it to be done with, no more working and practice. She told him the truth. He really needed that." Vonnegut's daughter Nanette continued, "I think it's partly what ruined my parents' marriage – her job as coach and him looking at her all those years while he's in labor." Nanette said the marriage was "fraying very, very badly before they divorced."[1] Vonnegut's temper was difficult for all in the household over the years. He often got angry when his writing was interrupted by noise or other disruptions. He was moody, grouchy, but he showed his love in other ways, such as days spent with the family laughing and enjoying the water at their house on Cape Cod.

Vonnegut's play "Happy Birthday, Wanda June" became a Broadway production. The opening night provided an opportunity for Vonnegut to meet the *Life* magazine photographer Jill Krementz. At an early age, the camera became a passion that took Krementz to notable current events of the time, including a trip to Vietnam capturing the war through images. She compiled an extensive collection of photographs of authors and was acquainted with a host of celebrities in New York City. When Vonnegut and Krementz met, they quickly fell in love, and Vonnegut moved to New York for the remainder of his life. Still, he occasionally returned to Barnstable, Indianapolis, and other locations for short and long getaways. His separation and eventual divorce from Jane was painful for the entire family, as Vonnegut chose to spend the last period of his life in a completely different way. He wanted to be a New Yorker.

"I wasn't stolen away by another woman. I don't think people can steal other people. I simply went away because the fighting was making everybody so unhappy. I've done that several times before. Going to Iowa was an example. Every time I went away I simply went to aloneness."[2]

While his love for Jane continued through her second marriage and untimely death from cancer in the 1980s, during the early 1970s, Vonnegut wanted to change the course of his life. He wanted to be "in love" again. He wanted the exciting social scene that celebrity life provided. He wanted to help students and up-and-coming writers. He wanted to continue writing. Like his parents, he wanted to be a big fish in a small pond – except his pond was The Big Apple rather than Indianapolis. Because of the success of *Slaughterhouse-Five*, he had the financial means to do nearly anything he wanted.

His wishes came true – along with challenges and pain. Vonnegut's years in New York were exciting at times but sometimes lonely, partly due to the melancholy he occasionally suffered throughout his life and partly because his second relationship proved not to be the unconditional love he had longed for all his adult life.

The 1970s were a whirlwind of activity, from the making of the movie version of *Slaughterhouse-Five* to the release of his first book since *Slaughterhouse-Five*, *Breakfast of Champions*. At the beginning of this decade, Vonnegut befriended Don and Annie Farber. Don, an attorney for Broadway stars and other celebrities, became Vonnegut's literary agent and all-around advisor. Don and Annie treated Vonnegut like a member of the family. Vonnegut signed on to the speaking circuit, appearing at numerous events from ACLU meetings to college graduations. During this decade he also released *Slapstick* and *Jailbird*. He became an outspoken supporter of the First Amendment during this period, as *Slaughterhouse Five* was banned in various venues in the United States and his friend and Russian translator Rita Rait was trying to defect from the Soviet Union because of censorship issues. "Free speech" became synonymous with Vonnegut. Through the 1960s and early 1970s, he spoke out with his folksy, Hoosier charm. His solid experience as a war veteran gave him credibility, for example, to speak out against the Vietnam War. He captured a national sentiment that he later included in his book *Bluebeard*:

> "Fathers are always so proud the first time they see their sons in uniform," she said. "I know Big John Karpinski was," I said. He is my neighbor to the north, of course. Big John's son Little John did badly in high school, and the police caught him selling dope. So he joined the Army while the Vietnam War was going on. And the first time he came home in uniform, I never saw Big John so happy, because it looked to him as though Little John was all straightened out and would amount to something. But then Little John came home in a body bag.[3]

Later in the 1970s, after cohabitating for a long while, Vonnegut wanted to show his love for Jill by marrying her. Vonnegut faced criticism from loved ones and strangers for this decision. The same people who would have celebrated him had he married a person of color or a person with a disability were among the first to practice agism by condemning him for marrying someone many years younger. In his defense, Vonnegut wrote to friends that Jill had helped him through this transition period of his life. Regarding the wedding itself, he wrote to his daughter Nanette: "It will be as secular as I can make it, since I am not a Christian of any kind. But it will take place in a church, because churches are so beautiful – and holy."[4] Before long, he wanted to give his young wife the opportunity to have a child of her own. The couple weathered storms, including miscarriage. Within months of the release of his book *Palm Sunday*, Vonnegut and Jill chose to become the proud parents of a baby girl, Lily.

In 1982, Vonnegut also met someone who became a dear friend and chronicler of his life. The young filmmaker Robert Weide entered into an agreement with Vonnegut to create a film about him. Weide worked with Kurt for years on a documentary film in which Weide traveled with Vonnegut throughout the country to capture the rich stories that occupied Vonnegut's mind. Released in 2021, the film titled *Kurt Vonnegut: Unstuck in Time* is not just about Vonnegut but also about Weide's life during the nearly 40 years spanning the making of the film.

The exciting moments of the 1980s brought the release of *Deadeye Dick, Galapagos,* and his friend Rita, who, after many years of trying, finally escaped the Iron Curtain and immigrated to the Netherlands. Vonnegut still found time to write letters to friends and ponder the themes that mattered throughout his life. In a letter to a high school friend, he wrote:

> I am now, because of my age and my steadfast lack of faith, at least a bishop in my own religion, German freethinking, and am, in fact, treated as a peer by the likes of Paul Moore [then Episcopal Bishop of New York], who has become one of my closest friends. I also get along fine with Jesuits. It wasn't until I was sixty-four [and] I came across a statement by Nietzsche that I could articulate why committed Christians and Jews sometimes find me respectable: "Only a person of deep faith can afford the luxury of skepticism."[5]

Deep faith in the companionship of various friends and advisors carried Vonnegut through another challenging period. On the anniversary of the firebombing of Dresden in February 1984 and overwhelmed by depression, Vonnegut intentionally overdosed on sleeping pills, once again showing the profound effect the war had on Vonnegut's psychological health. His friends the Farbers took him to the hospital, and he was cared for by his doctor for several weeks. Friends and family reached out to Vonnegut to express their support and love, and his daughter Edie ensured his peaceful transition from the hospital by leasing an apartment for him. "I'd go paint there with him during the day while he wrote," Edie recalled, "It was a nice time."

It took several years, in a collection of essays called *Fates Worse Than Death,* for Vonnegut to share his deeply personal thoughts on his family, depression, and suicide. Scholar Susan Farrell later wrote, "In *Fates Worse Than Death*, as in his novels, Vonnegut argues that people are at least partly bundles of chemical reactions. When a person's chemicals misfire, that person should be treated with sympathy and support, just as any physical illness would be treated."[6]

Vonnegut's daughter Nanette wrote, "Growing up, suicide was always considered a possible and even logical outcome of my father's life. But my father always answered the door, and I usually found him in the act of writing, which included working on the *New York Times* crossword puzzle."[7]

Entering yet another sad period of his life, Vonnegut's first wife, Jane, who had remarried years earlier, died from cancer in 1986. The two had had a friendly conversation prior to her death, but it was yet another difficult period to overcome. During this period, Vonnegut was working on the book *Bluebeard,* released in 1987. Vonnegut never "graded" this book the way he provided letter grades for his other works, but the *New York Times* said Bluebeard was a "minor achievement," moving Vonnegut neither backward nor forward in his writing career. Vonnegut fanatics – and some literary critics – loved this new work.

While Vonnegut continued to write, a number of his earlier works were still selling and some became films, including *Breakfast of*

Champions in 1988, with popular Hollywood actors of the time Bruce Willis and Nick Nolte leading the cast. Another earlier book was getting attention: a *Welcome to the Monkey House* short story "Who Am I This Time?" was turned into a film featuring celebrity actors Susan Sarandon and Christopher Walken. Meanwhile, the entire collection of stories was banned at a school in Ontario. Vonnegut wrote to the school principal condemning the action. The book's sales increased, as is often the case following acts of censorship.

Vonnegut juggled many activities and responsibilities but also enjoyed his time at a second home on Long Island, where the Vonneguts hosted lavish parties with neighbor friends, including John Irving, who had been his student at the Iowa Writers Workshop, and the celebrated author Truman Capote. Vonnegut began the 1990s with the release of *Hocus Pocus*. A *New York Times* reviewer said of that book: Vonnegut is "a satirist with a heart, a moralist with a whoopee cushion, a cynic who wants to believe."[8] While the book was not as highly regarded in the eyes of reviewers as his earlier work, his devoted fans devoured the book. On the home front, Vonnegut was busy being a dad and taking his youngest daughter, Lily, to summer camp and other activities. The demons he suffered from a life of challenges did not reveal themselves in his relationship with this child. Lily said, "Of course, the war affected him but not at any point in my entire life did I ever witness anything that set him off. Only kindness and love. He was the most present father who came to every sports game or musical I ever did. He drove me to camp every morning. As well to my friends – he was always there for them."[9]

Vonnegut was also busy writing, delivering speeches, and spending occasional time in Barnstable at the Vonnegut homestead with his daughter Edith and her family. Trying to fulfill the book deals his agent, Farber, had negotiated on his behalf, in 1991 Vonnegut published his often funny, often painful insights in *Fates Worse Than Death*. He wrote in the Preface that it was "a collection of essays and speeches by me, with breezy autobiographical commentary serving as connective tissue and splints and bandages. . .made to look like one big, preposterous animal not unlike an invention by Dr. Seuss."[10]

A random introduction at an event in Kentucky added an important new dimension to Vonnegut's life. A lifelong doodler with occasional paintings and sculptures sprinkled in, Vonnegut formalized his study of art when he met the artist Joe Petro III of Lexington, Kentucky. Petro and Vonnegut enjoyed each other's company and artistic talent so much that they decided to start a company together, called Origami Express. Vonnegut created art and Petro created silk screens of the art. They were in touch practically daily, despite the distance. This aspect of his life helped to stave off the loneliness that he experienced and also showed Vonnegut's ability to reach both into the literary arts and also the visual arts. He enjoyed featuring his work at gallery showings. Some fans are more familiar with Vonnegut's art than his books – but most know his art *because of* his books.

As Vonnegut was approaching his 75th birthday, he was writing *Timequake,* a novel that includes autobiographical information along with the theme of free will and time travel, again looking back like Lot's wife. That year, Vonnegut received an unexpected invitation to an event that would bring him peace. The body of his war buddy Ed Crone, the real-life model for Billy Pilgrim, was brought from Germany to Crone's hometown in upstate New York to be reinterred at a special ceremony. "Vonnegut visited Crones' grave, smoked a cigarette, spoke to Crone, and later said the encounter finally ended World War II for him."[11] Vonnegut had flowers placed on Crone's grave each Memorial Day until his own death and remained involved with the community in various ways.

The late 1990s brought a new traumatic experience in his life. Vonnegut's house caught on fire. As firefighters put out the flames, Vonnegut was taken to the emergency room, where it was determined he had suffered from smoke inhalation but would recover. Two years later, Vonnegut wondered if some of the same firemen who saved his life may have been among the victims of the September 11, 2001, terrorist attack on New York City. He spoke at a memorial service in the weeks that followed, reading off names of victims of the attacks on the World Trade Center. The events surrounding September 11th were personal for him as a New Yorker but also painful reminders of the citywide firestorm he survived in Dresden during the war. "Vonnegut's identification with these civil servants [firemen] was personal and deep-rooted. References to their constancy, professionalism and quiet heroics are a theme running throughout his half-century of novels and stories. Firemen symbolized for him the Midwestern ethic of neighborliness and mutual aid he had learned growing up in Indianapolis."[12] In his early book *Sirens of Titan*, Vonnegut wrote, *"I can think of no more stirring symbol of man's humanity to man than a fire engine."*[13]

Vonnegut enjoyed good times like going to the horse track, playing ping pong and tennis with New York buddies author Sidney Offit and broadcast journalist/reporter Morley Safer, and drinking with friends at his favorite bar. The years that followed September 11, 2001, were a concerning time for Vonnegut, due in part to his health but also to the state of the world. Vonnegut deplored the US attack on Iraq, which was falsely blamed for the September 11 terrorist attacks as a means for the Republican-majority Congress and president to lawfully send ground troops and Marines into combat. Vonnegut launched into his role of elder statesmen, a voice for yet another generation. He wrote columns for a publication called *In These Times* in which he discussed current events sprinkled with Vonnegutian references to Adam and Eve and characters in Greek mythology.

Invited by Mayor Bart Peterson to speak in Indianapolis in 2007 as part of a "Year of Vonnegut," Vonnegut was excited about the honor but less excited about the travel. He was tired. Still, he couldn't refuse an opportunity to come to back to his hometown. In his final years, Vonnegut became even more nostalgic about his childhood in Indianapolis. "Where is home? I've wondered where home is, and I realized, it's not Mars or someplace like that, it's Indianapolis when I was nine years old. I had a brother and a sister, a cat and a dog, and a mother and a father and uncles and aunts. And there's no way I can get there again."[14]

The speech Vonnegut intended to make in Indianapolis was written but never delivered. Soon before he was to travel to Indianapolis, Vonnegut tripped on his dog's leash coming down his front steps in New York and was knocked unconscious. He lapsed into a coma and finally passed away at age 84. Prophetically, in 1972 he had written in a letter to a friend: "I still believe that a dog is going to kill me, and it scares me – and it pisses me off."[15]

Fans everywhere mourned his loss. One conservative news source announced his death not by listing his achievements or even recognizing that he was a World War II veteran but by referring to him as a "failed suicide." Vonnegut likely would have had a hearty laugh at this comment, recognizing that he got under the skin of those he deemed harmful to the quality of life of others. Decades before, Martin Luther King Jr. said, "The true measure of a man is not how he behaves in moments of comfort and convenience but how he stands at times of controversy and challenges." Fans of Vonnegut awaited news of a funeral, but Vonnegut had long requested not to have a Christian burial. There are multiple stories regarding where his ashes are buried, some of which are colorful ones that reflect the humor and twists-and-turns of a Vonnegut short story. His memorial service was a private event held in New York, a loving tribute attended by friends and family.

Vonnegut gave us stories about individuals struggling for quality of life in an unjust world, about war and its collateral damage, about technologies that ruin lives, and many other topics to encourage his audience to develop wisdom and critical thinking skills, but to the end his stories also included humor and kindness. He left behind countless quotations that have helped people around the globe cope with the pandemic of 2020. Each of his devotees has a favorite Vonnegut quote. Nearing the end of his life, Vonnegut said this about himself and his fellow humans:

> Being merciful, it seems to me, is the only good idea we have received so far. Perhaps we will get another idea that good by and by – and then we will have two good ideas.[16]

Chapter Seven

Why Study Vonnegut?

Kurt Vonnegut's name regularly appears in listings of the greatest – most *celebrated* and *influential* – American authors. Beginning as a journalist, Vonnegut honed his writing style to include short sentences easily understood by all readers, making every word count. He is heralded for his courageous public speeches, essays, and newspaper columns, as well as his breadth of work – creating in his 50 years of published writing 14 novels, three collections of short stories, five plays, five works of nonfiction along with countless graduation speeches, letters, and more. His work appeared posthumously as researchers and family members sifted through his volumes of papers and unpublished writing.

Often pigeonholed as a political writer by some or a science-fiction writer by others, Vonnegut focused on commonalities among people – family, work, environment, nature, education, individual freedom and liberty, and the rights and safety of others. We study Vonnegut because his ability to understand the complex nature of war, economic systems, inequality, and behaviors that constitute common decency afforded him the opportunity to serve as spokesperson for his generation and new generations.

Vonnegut is seen by some as *counterculture*. In a tribute to the famous Beat poet, his friend Allen Ginsberg, Vonnegut wrote: "Allen Ginsberg and I were inducted into the American Institute of Arts and Letters in 1973. A reporter from *Newsweek* telephoned me at that time and asked me what I thought about two such outsiders being absorbed by the Establishment. I replied, "If we aren't the Establishment, I don't know who is."[1]

He did not see himself as counterculture, nor should his readers, although seeing him in that light satisfies a Vonnegut fan's need to be subversive. Vonnegut was, however, much more mainstream, an everyman, rather than a fringe thinker. He was considered a writer of the postmodernism movement of his era, skeptical of ideology and interested in improving the human condition. Still, Vonnegut was different even among this group because of his unique experiences and individual talents and interests. He could *not* be pigeonholed. His life and work made it acceptable for those with opinions contrary to the American agenda to voice their concerns. Like other artists during his generation, his use of his creative ability helped to move the country toward a more compassionate and progressive social agenda. He showed through his words and speeches the benefits of treating people not as pawns or property of corporate or government entities but as useful beings full of dignity, creativity, and perseverance, with the ability to love unconditionally if they so choose. "And, happily, an increasing number of general readers are finding in Vonnegut's quiet, humorous, well-mannered, and rational protests against man's inhumanity to man an articulate bridge across the generation chasm."[2]

We study Vonnegut to learn the craft of writing: careful choice of words, structure, and flow; the ability to accept constructive criticism; and the resilience and presence of mind to let go of unnecessarily harsh or unhelpful criticism. Vonnegut received dozens and dozens of rejection letters from magazines and book publishers. During his most productive and successful years as a writer, he was fortunate to have the dedication of an able editor, his first wife, Jane, whose contributions to his writing success cannot be overstated – both from the standpoint of editing and of doggedly reaching out to publishers on his behalf. Later, support for his work and through the difficult process of aging came from friends, his children, his second wife, Jill, his attorney, and publisher, among others.

While his early writing career included much rejection from publishers and their editors, Vonnegut's published work faced criticism from members of the literati as well as parents, school administrators, and school boards. One reason to study Vonnegut is because *Slaughterhouse-Five* is the most banned and challenged work that Vonnegut created, and banned books are usually worth reading. Reasons given for banning *Slaughterhouse-Five* include that it "contains foul language and promotes *deviant* sexual behavior," is "vulgar and offensive," is "rife with profanity and explicit sex," and "contains and makes references to religious matters."

Slaughterhouse-Five was burned in a high school furnace in Drake, North Dakota, which pained Vonnegut and led him to privately respond to the school principal, a letter that later became public and serves as an example to others of how to combat censorship.

With all of the book's vulgarity and profanity (the greatest of which, Vonnegut said, is the war itself) *Slaughterhouse-Five* was his catharsis. Like the Jester in the William Butler Yeats's poem "The Cap and Bells," Vonnegut presented his readership with his essence, his "cap and bells." And like the Queen in that poem, Vonnegut's audience of millions of readers responded with acclamation – love – for what he had created, recognizing what he and his family sacrificed in order for him to both remember and share with the world his horrific firsthand experience of war through the written word.

While Vonnegut's books are enlightening, we also study Vonnegut for his speeches, interviews, and essays, which provide insight, entertainment, and education. A casual reader may open a Vonnegut book to a page that includes a word or character that may be interpreted as offensive, vulgar, or just plain bothersome, but we must take the time to read his books. Readers are invited to put on their "full armor." Instead of attacking a "hot fudge sundae," readers are invited to learn more about what Vonnegut's words *mean* and what messages he was trying to convey. Vonnegut was a friend to the Civil Rights Movement, the Women's Movement, the movement for those with mental and physical disabilities, and the LGBTQ+ community, among others. In touch with these progressive movements of his long life, Vonnegut's work requires no apologies. Not only was he supportive, he served as a key voice in these movements locally, nationally, and globally. Vonnegut often wrote about what he knew about, which included protagonists in a male-dominated society, the societies with which Vonnegut was familiar as a soldier and as an employee of General Electric.

Vonnegut must remain connected with his moment in history. The morals he spent his life trying to teach people must be understood through a historical lens. For several decades, this concept of looking at historical and cultural context has been referred to as *new historicism*. The key to understanding art, literature, music, and more is not *censoring* creative people but instead *understanding* the era from which they came to better understand particular elements in their creative work. Artists historically serve as the conscience of society, not those who are dogmatically opposed to expanding the rights of others. Societies should strive to include *more* authors of different colors, races, ethnicities, and religions or lack of religion so that various experiences are represented from various eras rather than banning any individual who speaks from observations during a certain period. If readers separate Vonnegut from his era, his satirical words may be lost on them. They will be left out of the "party" that is Vonnegut – a party that is for all people.

Evidence that Vonnegut is among these social-justice minded individuals can also be found outside of his books, in his quotes and interviews such as one conducted by David Hoppe in 2003 in which Vonnegut said, "During the Vietnam War, which lasted longer than any war we've ever been in – and which we lost – every respectable artist in this country was against the war. It was like a laser beam. We were all aimed in the same direction. The power of this weapon turns out to be that of a custard pie dropped from a stepladder six feet high."[3]

Studying Vonnegut requires us to look inside his brain, from his study of anthropology and his life experiences, to selling Saabs at his car dealership, to creating a sculpture for $600 to bring art to passengers using Boston's Logan Airport. He believed that many of the world's problems existed because people did not understand other people. He had hope that if people did understand other people, we would like each other more and harm each other less.

Looking deeper into Vonnegut's brain, we learn what makes him tick, where his ideas come from, and what lessons we should consider. Vonnegut's use of the planet Tralfamadore and the Tralfamadorians was not just present in the book *Slaughterhouse-Five*. The planet is also referenced in *Sirens of Titan*; *God Bless You, Mr. Rosewater*; *Hocus Pocus*; and *Timequake*. As a little boy, Vonnegut looked to the night sky and pointed to his imaginary planet Tralfamadore. In many ways, Tralfamadore was his own Eden, the place he could escape to in his mind where inhabitants were higher level beings, happier than humans. Tralfamadorians were "higher level" because they were more knowledgeable about the science of nature. What may seem like exaggerations to readers was Vonnegut's way of telling readers that humans don't know enough about each other and other life forms.

In addition to studying Vonnegut for his words and his moral teachings, we should study Vonnegut because of his life. What can be learned from his life? When readers study Vonnegut's life, we learn things he may not have known about himself. He didn't share all of his thoughts with friends and family, especially thoughts about the war experience, but he sometimes shared his thoughts through dialogue and countless volumes of correspondence. Social scientists, biographers, and the average reader are able to see patterns. For example, many believe *Slaughterhouse-Five* serves as an example of Vonnegut writing about those who suffered from mental health challenges, specifically, post-traumatic stress disorder (PTSD). Military officials, lower-level officers, and enlisted ranks historically discriminated and encouraged discrimination of those service members who were suffering mental health challenges. As one military official wrote to a newspaper in 1919: "No one should be permitted to glorify himself as a case of 'shell shock.' It should become widely known that a persistent war neurosis is not something of which to be proud. It is not the same as an honorable wound."[4]

Vonnegut was never officially diagnosed by a mental health expert with PTSD. Some scholars, friends, and family say he obviously suffered from the condition. Others say he showed no signs.

Why is it important to further explore and try to understand this aspect of Vonnegut? Because studying him may help with the unanswered questions regarding trauma. His life can teach us something that may help other families understand how to help and cope with individuals who have suffered trauma.

We study Vonnegut to understand the countless Vonnegut fans who have said, "Kurt Vonnegut saved my life. I was reading his books, and it seemed like he understood exactly what I was going through." Vonnegut connected with his readers on a personal level. When people read Vonnegut, they are acquiring not just a story but also a friend. He was unusual because he included himself in many of his books – literally speaking in first person as a narrator-character. Narrators don't typically do this. For the books where he wasn't speaking in first-person, he was still present as an unusual, silly, alien, or generally foolish character who ultimately was the wisest person in the book, the voice people most needed to hear because of the wisdom these characters imparted.

We study Vonnegut to chronicle the history of various movements. In addition to soldiers, prisoners were another category of individual to whom Vonnegut drew attention. In *Player Piano*, "Harrison Bergeron," and *Slaughterhouse-Five*, Vonnegut included social commentary on prisoners and prisons. He saw himself as a fellow prisoner. Vonnegut wasn't concerned only with the mental health of prisoners but also the prison industrial complex. He was aware that America ranks third in the world by population for the number of people in prison. Mass incarceration weighed heavily on his mind.

What troubles me most about my lovely country is that its children are seldom taught that American freedom will vanish, if, when they grow up, and in the exercise of their duties as citizens, they insist that our courts and policemen and prisons be guided by divine or natural law.[5]

Vonnegut also advocated for women's rights. In an article titled "Vonnegut Hails the 'Dignity of Women,'" *New York Times* author Alvin Klein wrote in 1989 that for decades Vonnegut was "espousing feminist and pacifist causes, as well as anti-Establishment and pro-humanist attitudes."[6]

Readers of fiction are not always readers of philosophy or theology. Vonnegut used his protagonists Paul Proteus, Harrison Bergeron, and Billy Pilgrim to highlight, as philosopher Joseph Campbell put it, "the validity of the individual's experience of what humanity is, what life is, what values are, against the monolithic system."[7]

Terms used by individuals over the years to describe Vonnegut include *curmudgeon, cantankerous, sour, impatient,* and *cold,* but equally kind words have been used, such as *hopeful, loving, funny, caring, brave, reliable, optimistic,* and *generous.* Having survived the deaths of his mother, Joe Crone, his sister and brother-in-law, and many fellow ser-vicemembers, friends, and family members over the years, Vonnegut's life and philosophy could be described as the approach of a "Pyrrhic victory." Pyrrhus of Epirus was a great military commander that Vonne-gut studied. Pyrrhus took on the Romans in multiple battles between 280 and 275 BCE. He is famous for saying, "If we are victorious in one more battle with the Romans, we shall be utterly ruined." Having lost key leaders and thousands of soldiers, his predictions of the outcomes of future conquests are often referred to as simply "winning the battle but losing the war." Vonnegut wrote at the end of *Slaughterhouse-Five* that the book is a failure, and it "had to be." Some critics have misun-derstood his intent with this statement. It is in fighting the battles and celebrating the victories that makes life worthwhile. Sometimes celebrating the victories can be as simple as recognizing life's simple pleasures. In *A Man Without a Country*, Vonnegut wrote:

> But I had a good uncle, my late Uncle Alex. He was my father's kid brother, a childless graduate of Harvard who was an honest life-insurance sales-man in Indianapolis. He was well-read and wise. And his principal complaint

about other human beings was that they so seldom noticed it when they were happy. So when we were drinking lemonade under an apple tree in the summer, say, and talking lazily about this and that, almost buzzing like honeybees, Uncle Alex would suddenly interrupt the agreeable blather to exclaim, "If this isn't nice, I don't know what is." So I do the same now, and so do my kids and grandkids. And I urge you to please notice when you are happy, and exclaim or murmur or think at some point, "If this isn't nice, I don't know what is."[8]

Vonnegut's friend Tracy Goss, an actress turned author and expert in the field of executive leadership training, explained something that Vonnegut knew as a young man: "When you accept that life does not turn out the way it "should," you are free to take actions that are not constrained by the need to control life so it turns out the way that it "should" (or, at the very least, to make sure life doesn't turn out the way it "shouldn't").[9]

Vonnegut studied the social sciences. He created new religions in his fiction, revealing his knowledge of theology and anthropology to entertain but also to challenge religious and social conventions. He said: "The creator of the Universe has been to us unknowable so far. We serve as well as we can the highest abstraction of which we have some understanding, which is our community."[10]

Those who study Vonnegut are part of a large community – whether they participate in virtual or in-person events at the Kurt Vonnegut Museum and Library or through music, comedy, theater, or other performances that regularly happen in large and small towns all over the world. Vonnegut made up a word to describe this type of community and used the term in his book *Cat's Cradle*. That term is *karass*.

We study Vonnegut because part of the global Vonnegut karass means that people follow Vonnegut's roadmap to having a happy life, despite setbacks, if we engage in and practice the following: gratitude, tenderness, thoughtful dialogue, extended families, meaningful work, and humor. Vonnegut's humor kept him alive in the worst of times and comforts his readers during their difficult times. When a researcher asked Vonnegut "if he had his choice, what he would most like to be remembered as, Vonnegut answered, 'George Orwell.'"[11] Orwell, another giant in the realm of authors focused on social criticism, outsold Vonnegut with regard to numbers of books but was not as prolific as Vonnegut. Orwell, brilliant for his creative output, is not remembered as a *friend* to the reader in the unique way that Vonnegut was or *is*. Orwell had said "every joke is a tiny revolution." Vonnegut's humor, which surpassed Orwell's, was a series of revolutions. He was, like Lot's wife in the Bible story, our *witness*. He was our *pillar of salt* and at the same time, our hot fudge sundae. His most important message was the one he wrote to newborns:

> *Hello babies. Welcome to Earth. It's hot in the summer and cold in the winter. It's round and wet and crowded. On the outside, babies, you've got a hundred years here. There's only one rule that I know of, babies –"God damn it, you've got to be kind."*[12]

Notes

CHAPTER ONE

1. Vonnegut, Kurt. 1998. *Timequake*. New York: Berkeley.
2. Vonnegut, Kurt, and Vonnegut, Edith. 2020. *Love, Kurt: The Vonnegut Love Letters 1941-1945*. New York: Random House
3. Vonnegut, Kurt. 1999. *Wampeters, Foma, and Grandfalloons*. New York: Dial Press.
4. McCartan, Tom. 2011. *Vonnegut: The Last Interview and Other Stories*. New York: Melville House.
5. Vonnegut, Kurt, and Wakefield, Dan. 2014. *Kurt Vonnegut: Letters*. New York: Dial Press.
6. Vonnegut, Kurt. 2007. *A Man Without a Country*. New York: Random House.
7. Vonnegut, Kurt, and McConnell, Suzanne. *Pity the Reader: On Writing with Style*. 2019. New York: Seven Stories Press.
8. Vonnegut, Kurt and Brancaccio, David. 2005, October 7. *Now with David Brancaccio*. PBS.
9. Vonnegut, Kurt. 1986, 24 February. McFadden Lecture. North Central High School, Indianapolis, Indiana.
10. Leeds, Marc. 2016. *The Vonnegut Encyclopedia*. New York: Delacorte.
11. Vonnegut, Kurt. *Bagombo Snuff Box*.

CHAPTER TWO

1. Vonnegut, Kurt, and Vonnegut, Edith. 2020. *Love, Kurt: The Vonnegut Love Letters 1941-1945*. New York: Random House.
2. Shields, Charles. 2011. *And So It Goes: Kurt Vonnegut: A Life*. New York: Henry Holt and Co.
3. Vonnegut and Vonnegut, 2020.
4. Ibid.
5. Roston, Tom. 2021. *The Writer's Crusade: Kurt Vonnegut and the Many Lives of Slaughterhouse-Five*. New York: Abrams Press.
6. Vonnegut and Vonnegut, 2020.
7. Ibid.
8. Vonnegut, Kurt. *Mother Night*. 1961 (reissued 2009). New York: Dial Press.
9. Shields, Charles. 2011. *And So It Goes: Kurt Vonnegut: A Life*. New York: Henry Holt and Co.
10. Roston, 2021.
11. Vonnegut, Kurt, and Vonnegut, Nanette. 2014. *Kurt Vonnegut: Drawings*. New York: the Monacelli Press.
12. Vonnegut, Kurt. 1999. *Palm Sunday*. New York: Dial Press.
13. Leeds, Marc. 2016. *The Vonnegut Encyclopedia*. New York: Delacorte.
14. Vonnegut, Kurt, and Wakefield, Dan. 2016. *If This Isn't Nice, What Is? (Much) Expanded Second Edition: The Graduation Speeches and Other Words to Live By*. New York: Seven Stories Press.

CHAPTER THREE

1. Vonnegut, Kurt, and Wakefield, Dan. 2014. *Kurt Vonnegut: Letters*. New York: Dial Press.
2. Ibid.
3. Allen, William Rodney. 1991. *Understanding Kurt Vonnegut*. Columbia: University of South Carolina Press.

4. Vonnegut, Kurt. Reprinted 1999. *Player Piano*. New York: Dial Press.
5. Ibid.
6. Ibid.
7. Ibid.
8. Ibid.
9. Ibid.
10. Ibid.
11. Hicks. 1952. Player Piano. *New York Times*. 17 August, www.nytimes.com/1952/08/17/books/vonnegut-player.html

CHAPTER FOUR

1. Vonnegut, Kurt. 2010. *Welcome to the Monkey House*. New York: Dial Press.
2. Houpt, Simon. 2005. The World According to Kurt. *Toronto Globe and Mail*. 11 October. https://www.theglobeandmail.com/arts/the-world-according-to-kurt/article18250184/
3. Vonnegut, Kurt. 2010. *Welcome to the Monkey House*. New York: Dial Press.
4. Ibid.
5. Ibid.
6. Rothschild, Scott. 2005. Vonnegut: Lawyers Could Use Literary Lesson. *Lawrence Journal-World*. 5 May. www2.ljworld.com/news/2005/may/05/vonnegut_lawyers_could/
7. Ibid.

CHAPTER FIVE

1. Montagne, Renee. 2003. Kurt Vonnegut: A Free-Thinking American. NPR: All Things Considered. 10 September.
2. Vonnegut, Kurt. 1991. *Slaughterhouse-Five*. New York: Dell.
3. Ibid.
4. Ibid.

5. Ibid.
6. Ibid.
7. Ibid.
8. Longfellow, Henry Wadsworth. 1860. "Paul Revere's Ride." https://poets.org/poem/paul-reveres-ride
9. Marvin, Thomas. 2002. *Kurt Vonnegut: A Critical Companion*. Westport, CT: Greenwood Press.
10. Longfellow, 1860.
11. Vonnegut, 1991.
12. McRae, John. 1915. "In Flanders Fields." www.poetry-foundation.org/poems/47380/in-flanders-fields
13. Kramer, D. 2019. Kurt Vonnegut's 1995 "Billy Pilgrim" Pilgrimage to the Mt. Hope Grave of Edward R. Crone Jr., Brighton High School '4. *Talker of the Town*. 8 March. https://talkerofthetown.com/2019/03/08/kurt-vonneguts-1995-billy-pilgrim-pilgrimage-the-mt-hope-grave-of-edward-crone-jr-brighton-high-school-41/
14. Kauffman, Bill. 2019. Slaughterhouse-Five and HWS Alum Remembered. *The WHS Update*. Hobart and William Smith Colleges. 9 October. https://www2.hws.edu/slaughterhouse-five-and-hws-alum-remembered/
15. Vonnegut, 1991.
16. Marvin, 2002.
17. Vonnegut, 1991.
18. Ibid.
19. Wakefield, Dan. Christ Loving Atheist. *Image Journal*. https://imagejournal.org/article/kurt-vonnegut/
20. Marvin, 2002.
21. 1969. Slaughterhouse-Five or the Children's Crusade. *New York Times*. 31 March. https://www.nytimes.com/1969/03/31/books/vonnegut-slaughterhouse.html
22. Ibid.
23. Vonnegut, Kurt, and Wakefield, Dan. 2014. *Kurt Vonnegut: Letters*. New York: Dial Press.

CHAPTER SIX

1. Bowen, Jennifer. 2012. 12 November. The Rumpus Interview with Nanette Vonnegut. The Rumpus
2. Vonnegut, Kurt, and Wakefield, Dan. 2014. *Kurt Vonnegut: Letters*. New York: Dial Press
3. Vonnegut, Kurt. 2011. *Bluebeard*. New York: Dial Press.
4. Vonnegut and Wakefield, 2014.
5. Wakefield, Dan. "Christ-Loving Atheist." *Image Journal*. https://imagejournal.org/article/kurt-vonnegut/
6. Farrell, Susan. 2008. *Critical Companion to Kurt Vonnegut: A Literary Reference to His Life and Work*. New York: Facts on File.
7. Vonnegut, Kurt. 2012. *We Are What We Pretend to Be: The First and Last Works*. Vanguard Press. New York.
8. McInerney, Jay. 1990. September 9. "Still Asking the Embarrassing Questions: Hocus Pocus by Kurt Vonnegut." *New York Times Book Review*.
9. Vonnegut, Lily, and Whitehead, Julia. 2021. 25 July. Email exchange.
10. Vonnegut, Kurt. 1991. *Fates Worse Than Death*. G.P. Putnam's Sons. New York.
11. Kauffman, Bill. 2019. 9 October. Slaughterhouse Five and HWS Alum Remembered. *The WHS Update*. Hobart and William Smith Colleges. https://www2.hws.edu/slaughterhouse-five-and-hws-alum-remembered/
12. Donahue, Allison. 2011. 11 September. Vonnegut's Firefighters. *The New Inquiry*. https://thenewinquiry.com/vonneguts-firefighters/
13. Vonnegut, Kurt. 1998. *Sirens of Titan*. New York: Dial Press.
14. Gunderman, Richard. 2021. Indy Beacons: Vonnegut Family Had Multi-Generational Influence on City. *Indianapolis Business Journal*. 4 June https://www.ibj.com/articles/vonnegut-family-had-multi-generational-influence-on-the-city

15. Vonnegut and Wake-field, 2014.

16. Ibid.

CHAPTER SEVEN

1. Allen, William Rodney. 1991. *Understanding Kurt Vonnegut*. Columbia: University of South Carolina Press.

2. Vonnegut, Kurt, and Wake-field, Dan. 2014. *Kurt Von-negut: Letters*. New York: Dial Press.

3. Hoppe, David, and Vonnegut, Kurt. Vonnegut at 80: I'm Mad About Being Old and I'm Mad About Being American. 2003 *NUVO* 1 January. https://nuvo.newsnirvana.com/news/news/vonnegut-at-80/article_04fdbc54-9435-54aa-992c-3130443dc334.html

4. Roston, Tom. 2021. *The Writer's Crusade: Kurt Von-negut and the Many Lives of Slaughterhouse-Five*. New York: Abrams Press.

5. Vonnegut, Kurt. 1999. *Palm Sunday*. New York: Dial Press.

6. Klein, Alvin. 1989. Vonnegut Hails the "Dignity of Women." *New York Times*. 27 August.

7. Moyers, Bill. 1988. Joseph Campbell and the Power of Myth: The "Hero's Adventure." 21 June. Billmoyers.com.

8. Vonnegut and Wakefield, 2014.

9. Goss, Tracy. 2015. *The Last Word on Power*. Rosetta Books, LLC.

10. Vonnegut and Wake-field, 2014.

11. Allen, 1991.

12. Vonnegut, Kurt. *God Bless You, Mr. Rosewater*. 1998. New York: Dial Press.

Index

Praise for
Breaking Down Vonnegut

"Reading Kurt Vonnegut's books in high school English classes helped spark my love of reading."
   —John Green, author of *The Fault in Our Stars* and *The Anthropocene Reviewed*

"Julia Whitehead's daily commitment to raising awareness about Kurt Vonnegut – the man, the thinker, the writer – shines through as she connects his literary legacy to the social and political issues we confront today. She helps us see how Vonnegut's deeply rooted Midwestern values inform his vision for a more just and equal society."
   —A'Lelia Bundles, author of *On Her Own Ground: The Life and Times of Madam C. J. Walker*

"Vonnegut remains the most fascinating human I have ever interviewed. Whitehead's account is a useful and accessible introduction to the life of a cultural giant."
   —David Brancaccio, public radio and TV journalist

"What a breath of fresh air is Julia Whitehead's *Breaking Down Vonnegut*—erudite yet unassuming, free of nonsense. This is a book on Kurt Vonnegut that Kurt Vonnegut himself would have loved."
   —Dan Simon, editor of Kurt Vonnegut's *A Man without a Country* and co-author of *Run Run Run: The Lives of Abbie Hoffman*

"This is a wonderfully clear, humane, and witty introduction to Vonnegut's life and work. If you didn't already love and appreciate this particular human, Whitehead will make you a believer."
   —Dave Eggers, author of *The Every*

"Of Julia Whitehead's many insights into Kurt and his work, this meant the most to me: that his greatest achievement was serving as a propagandist for peace."
   —James Thorn